"Miss Newby, you're a fool!"

The harsh words broke the still night to echo Kathy's thoughts. Startled, she whirled and searched the darkness for the source, even as she recognized Jared's voice. He crossed the distance between them with a grace unusual in such a large man.

"Why, Mr. Jarrett . . . to what do I owe this unprofessional analysis?" she asked, as the hot tears burned behind her eyes.

"Dinner tonight was a disaster because you acted the part of a spineless fool," he scoffed. "Alana was a positive cat, and you took it all without so much as a whimper. What's the matter with you? Don't you have any self-respect? . . . You probably earned a few points with mother—but you lost as many with me! She would approve of your Christian performance, but the only thing that impressed me was your ability to 'turn the other cheek' so many times without suffering whiplash!"

When he finally paused to take another drag on his cigarette, Kathy spoke softly. "I probably could have won your respect instead of your contempt. But, since our values are so different, perhaps I should consider it a compliment to be labeled a fool by your standards. Two wrongs don't make a right, you know."

Jared turned away uncomfortably, sensing a Presence within her, a greater Power that gave Katherine Newby strength even when she was outnumbered. When she looked up at him, her innocent face lovely in the pale moonlight, Jared Jarrett felt lost, uncertain. He was desperately aware of a need to escape her, just as he was helplessly drawn to her, and all she represented.

LOVE'S SWEET PROMISE

Susan C. Feldhake

BOOKS

of the Zondervan Publishing House
Grand Rapids, Michigan

Other Serenade Books by Susan C. Feldhake

For Love Alone

LOVE'S SWEET PROMISE
Copyright © 1983 by Susan C. Feldhake

Library of Congress Cataloging in Publication Data

Feldhake, Susan C.
    Love's sweet promise.
    I. Title.
PS3556.E4575L6   1983   813'.54   83-6930
ISBN 0-310-46462-5

Edited by Anne Severance
Designed by Kim Koning

Printed in the United States of America

83 84 85 86 87 88 89 / 10 9 8 7 6 5 4 3 2 1

For my lovely daughter, Marie,
whose tears became my treasures of belief.

CHAPTER 1

KATHERINE NEWBY STEERED her small borrowed car carefully through the early summer storm. Angry streaks of lightning stabbed the black sky, and the streets were rushing freshets. Her concentration was broken by the lively chatter of her three friends.

"Wasn't the symphony wonderful?" Trish Nobel, Kathy's roommate and a fellow schoolteacher, bubbled from the back seat. Trish, an ardent connoisseur of the arts, had persuaded the entire faculty of Miss Atwood's Academy for Young Women to attend the opening night of the city's famed symphony series and was elated with the standing-room-only crowd in the civic auditorium.

A crack of thunder jolted the women's attention to the dark sky.

"We're almost there," Kathy sighed gratefully, catching sight of the heavily wooded Atwood Avenue. She turned onto the Academy's long drive. Instantly all eyes were riveted on the unbelievable sight before them. Kathy's foot involuntarily released the gas pedal and her hands gripped the wheel for support. The car slowed to a halt.

"Oh, *no*!" Trish cried in disbelief.

They could see faintly, at the end of the circular drive, that the once stately mansion, lately an exclusive girls' school covering an entire city block, lay in smoldering ruins. A half-dozen fire trucks, parked randomly around the building, were adding pounding jets of spray to the pouring rain. Brick tumbled upon smoke-blackened brick. Stark chimneys thrust skyward from mounds of burning embers. Giant maples and oaks—their bark charred, their leaves scorched and curled from the intense heat—drooped despairingly above the rubble.

Kathy managed to compose herself long enough to pull up the drive to allow room for the other cars which would be returning from the symphony hall.

"Thank God that we are all safe—and that the fire didn't strike during a school day," she sighed heavily.

In their hotel room Trish sank to the beige chenille bedspread and kicked off her high-heeled shoes, not bothering to undo the straps. She rubbed her aching insteps and raked her fingers through her long flaxen hair while Kathy hung up her evening coat.

"Well, Kath, old girl, the big question: What are we going to do now?"

"I don't know about you, Trish," she said, yawning, "but I'm going to look for a job first thing in the morning." Checking her watch, she found that it was already well past midnight. "Right now, though, I'm going to get some sleep."

Trish rolled her eyes and made an affectionate face at her friend.

"I can't believe you! You sound as if you hadn't just lost everything you own in the world. Kathy, you have nothing left, except the clothes on your back. Yet you talk as though you had everything!"

Kathy smiled as she unzipped the blue dress—an exact match for large, deep-set eyes. She had always considered them her best feature, though Trish envied her short, naturally curly black hair which required little more than a quick brushing to fall fetchingly into place around an oval face.

"I do have everything I really need, Trish—except a job. Lord willing, that problem will be solved shortly. But if I don't find something soon, I'll get by somehow. Things will work out. They do, if you have faith."

Lying in bed that night, Kathy thought about Trish's remark. It was true that she had nothing left . . . nothing of material value. Trish herself had a large, generous family nearby and a sizable bank account. She would be all right.

The insurance company had called the fire at the Academy "an act of God." But Kathy Newby's God did not destroy—He comforted and sustained, didn't He? Even with her belief in His loving presence during the past difficult months, the petite, dark-haired girl had struggled to understand a punishing onslaught of circumstances that might have quenched the strongest faith.

First, her father's accident. Then, her mother's lingering illness and death. Now this! Without self-pity Kathy pondered her troubled past and nebulous future. Luckily the local realtor in her hometown in southern Illinois had been able to sell the Newby residence almost immediately after it had been put up for sale after her mother's funeral. But by the time all the debts were paid, and the lawyer's fees and real estate agent's commission deducted, there was precious little left. Kathy's own resources, accumulated since her graduation from college, had steadily dwindled, eroded by frequent visits home before the final trip to bury her mother. Katherine Newby was, at the moment, practically penniless!

As the ashes cooled, a benumbed Mary Ann Atwood— *the* Miss Atwood—had assured her faculty that fire insurance would cover all personal items. But, she had warned, the money probably wouldn't be forthcoming for several more days.

"Weeks! Months! Good grief—maybe even *years!*" Trish had groaned, giving Kathy a dismal look. "You know how some insurance companies can be, Kath. They're Johnny-on-the-spot when it comes to collecting premiums, but turtle-slow when settling claims."

9

"I hope not," sighed Kathy, although she realized that what her friend said was probably true. Then she turned over, breathed a fervent prayer of gratitude for their safety, and slept dreamlessly.

When the girl at the switchboard rang room 402 at seven o'clock the next morning, Kathy felt as if she had barely closed her eyes. The signal also awakened Trish, who sleepily crawled out of bed to put through a call to her parents in Kansas City. She wanted to break the news to them before they learned about the fire from a newscast. When she replaced the receiver, she made plans to go downtown to shop for some clothes, while Kathy dialed an employment agency and made an appointment for a job interview.

"I feel like an idiot being seen in public at this hour of the morning in this get-up," Trish muttered, after she had showered and dressed.

Kathy regarded her and laughed. She felt silly enough in her own evening attire, which was subdued in comparison to Trish's flamboyant outfit.

Her friend leaned over, secured the strap of her shoe, and gave Kathy a warning frown. "And don't tell me about the lilies of the field, either."

"I don't have to, pal," Kathy grinned. "It seems you just reminded yourself!"

Trish laughed lightly, then reached for the coat she had draped over a chair. "Are you sure you won't come with me? Misery loves company, you know!"

"Don't tempt me, Trish. It isn't nice," Kathy cautioned. "Besides, first things first."

The two girls boarded the city bus at a corner stop. When Kathy got off to walk the remaining blocks to the Archway Employment Agency, Trish gave her a wave and an encouraging smile and promised to see her later in the day.

Kathy's high heels clicked with a staccato tap on the cement sidewalk. The delicate shoes were torturous to walk in, and she was relieved when she spotted the agency just ahead. She hurried to the door and stepped inside, only to be confronted by the receptionist's reproachful stare.

"May I help you?" she inquired crisply. Kathy glanced at the nametag which read *Sylvia Browning*. The woman regarded her from head to toe.

Kathy's vivid teal blue silk evening dress set her painfully apart from the more modestly dressed applicants.

"I called for an appointment earlier this morning. I—I'm looking for a job," Kathy murmured, her voice thin and breathless from the brisk walk. "But then I suppose most of the people you meet are looking for work," she added with a nervous laugh.

Miss Browning was clearly not amused. "And what kind of work did you have in mind . . . Miss . . ."

"Newby. Katherine Newby," she offered, as the receptionist poised a pen over a printed form which she had extracted from a drawer beneath the counter.

"Newby," she echoed, filling in the first line with a flourish.

"I'm qualified to teach," Kathy said. "But I'll consider something else. I really need the income . . ."

Miss Browning silenced Kathy with a glance. Her tired expression suggested that she had heard it all before, many times. "We do the best we can." Her forced smile was a rebuke. "But of course, we can make no promises."

"I understand," Kathy sighed, feeling chastened. "It's just that until very recently—last night, in fact—I was employed as a teacher. At Miss Atwood's Academy for Young Women."

Miss Browning's demeanor changed instantly. Her brown eyes, which had been aloof and impenetrable, softened, coming alive with sympathy. She appeared to sniff the air, as if expecting to detect the lingering scent of smoke. Now she understood why such a pretty girl— obviously intelligent, cultured, and well-mannered—was so inappropriately dressed. The morning newspapers and telecasts had captured the demise of the grand old estate as it burned to the ground. The cause, as yet undetermined, was under investigation by the city fire marshall.

Miss Browning bit her lip and clucked in sympathy. "Such a tragedy, Miss Newby."

Turning her attention to the sheaf of papers before her, she noted Kathy's concise answers on the forms. "You're very well qualified," she observed. Managing a tight little smile, she placed the papers in a folder. "Please be seated. One of our counselors will be with you soon. Perhaps we will have an opening for you. If not, we get new listings every day. Something will turn up."

"Thank you."

Kathy took a chair in the corner of the tastefully decorated waiting room. Nearby was a well-stocked magazine rack, but she had no interest in the periodicals. She leaned back, closing her eyes.

Everyone had commented that the fire at the Academy was a tragedy, and, in many ways, it was. With a faith that many people found naïve, Kathy believed that God never allowed such things to happen unless He intended to use the trying experiences to serve His purposes. Furthermore, she fully expected to discover in time that the "tragedy" had been a blessing in disguise. Just how and when, of course, remained to be seen.

Teaching was a career Kathy loved. As an instructor, she went far beyond the job description, both in and out of the classroom. At times, she realized, she had devoted almost as much of her time and energy to the Academy as Miss Atwood herself! This dedication had not escaped the notice of Mary Ann Atwood. It was solid proof that the elderly woman's decision to employ Katherine Newby, despite her youth and lack of experience, was well founded. While Miss Atwood rejoiced in her good fortune, Trish Nobel was dismayed.

"Katherine Newby, I'm so furious with you!" Trish cried one Saturday evening as she dressed for a dinner date. "You're going to wind up an old maid—just like Miss Atwood—if you don't watch your step! Keep it up, and, when she dies, you can buy this Victorian relic and call it 'Miss Newby's School for the Daughters of the Filthy

Rich.' The fine old tradition will be carried on. Then, years from now, when you are old and senile, you can pass on the torch—and maybe the mortgage—to some other sweet, dedicated young thing *you* can brag about having the foresight to have hired!''

Trish's humorous and fervent tirade made Kathy laugh. ''Just because I don't go out every weekend doesn't guarantee I'm going to be a spinster.''

''Maybe not,'' Trish granted, as she leaned toward her magnifying mirror and smoothed an eyebrow. ''But you've already got a darned good start. Why . . .'' Trish's eyes narrowed in thought. ''*I* can't even remember the last time you were out with a guy. *Can you*?''

''Of course I can!'' she protested. Her brows furrowed in a frown as her thoughts spun back over the weeks, then the months. Trish restrained herself from chortling over what was apparent from Kathy's expression. She *couldn't* recall her last date!

''Most of the time when you 'go out'—and I'm using the term very loosely—it's to the museum, the St. Louis Zoo, shopping with me, or to a movie with another staffer from the Academy. Kathy, I don't want to seem meddlesome, but you're much too pretty to wilt on the vine. I want to get married someday and have a family. I'll bet you do, too. But you'll never meet eligible men hiding out in our room on the third floor of Miss Atwood's Academy. You have to go places if you're hoping to find Mr. Right. And,'' Trish's face grew dismal at the thought, ''sift through a lot of Mr. Wrongs in the process.''

Kathy wanted to tell Trish she wasn't interested in beating the bushes. She had the calm assurance that when she met the right man, she would know it, as would he.

''We're going to do something about this situation,'' Trish announced in a no-nonsense voice. ''I'm going to ask Charlie to find a friend for you.'' Trish leaned over Kathy's shoulder and studied the small desk calendar. ''Ahhh . . . good! You don't have anything planned for next Saturday,'' Trish said. She grabbed Kathy's pen, and marked the date with a large X. "Now you do, dearie. You're going out with us and one of Charlie's friends."

"But—"

"No buts about it, Kathy. We *are* going. Period. End of subject. It'll be fun."

The following weekend, Kathy did join Trish and Charlie, and their friend Brad, a young lawyer who had just signed on with a large, prestigious St. Louis firm.

As Trish had promised, Kathy enjoyed the evening. Trish was pleased with herself and Kathy suspected that under her friend's ample bosom beat the heart of a matchmaker. Later, back at the Academy, Trish was disappointed to learn that Kathy hadn't fallen instantly, utterly, and hopelessly in love with the handsome attorney.

" 'Nice?' Merely *'nice'?* Is that *all* you can say about Brad Mathews?" Trish was horrified. "Good grief, Kath. Brad's one of the most eligible bachelors in the city. Lots of women would give an arm to have a date with him. Brad's got it all—looks, brains, a job with incredible potential, and his family has pots and pots of money. Brad could give you anything your little heart could desire."

"No, he could not," Kathy started to say. But she bit back the words and shrugged.

It was useless to try to explain to Trish that, while Brad Mathews had a great deal to offer, he couldn't give Kathy the one thing she wanted most—the love and lifestyle of a committed Christian. Without a faith to match her own, whatever Brad could give would never be enough.

"Mr. Stockton will see you now, Miss Newby," the receptionist summoned, interrupting her reverie.

Sylvia Browning favored Kathy with a wide smile and led her down the short hallway to a door opening into a sunny, private office.

A short, rotund man, with curly brown hair and snapping brown eyes behind horn-rimmed glasses, smiled pleasantly and rose to greet her. He motioned for her to take the chair across from his desk.

14

"Miss Browning told me about your predicament, Miss Newby. A blow to you, I'm sure."

"Yes, it has been," Kathy replied.

Mr. Stockton examined her qualifications. "I suppose you'd prefer a position similar to the one you held at Miss Atwood's?"

"I'd accept a position in a private school if there were an opening immediately. Otherwise I'd really prefer something not so cloistered," Kathy replied, remembering Trish's lectures.

"Unfortunately there are no area private schools currently in need of a teacher. With only a few weeks to go before the term ends, most teachers can arrange to finish out the year."

"That's why I'm prepared to consider anything, even something outside my field."

Mr. Stockton's smile was patient. "We prefer to place people where they're best qualified. It makes for satisfied clients." He riffled through the catalog of listings. "What about tutoring?"

"Well . . ."

Kathy was hesitant. In her senior year at Eastern Illinois University she had worked as a tutor to defray her college expenses. There had been no shortage of children in the general area who needed a bit of extra help. The tutoring jobs had been rewarding enough, but the pay had not compared with her most recent salary. Also tutoring all too often meant evening hours, which presented a transportation problem, the prospects of traveling lonely, dark streets alone.

"I would consider tutoring," Kathy acquiesced. "But only very close by, and then only until I could find something more satisfactory—and permanent."

Mr. Stockton sighed as he looked over the listings. "I'd like to keep you in teaching. But, if we can't . . . say, here's one!" He stabbed the listing with his index finger. As he read, his face brightened, then clouded in disappointment. "This is a temporary teaching job, private tutoring, with a chance for permanency. But I don't think you would be interested . . ."

Kathy wasn't so sure. "I might be."

"It's out of the area. South Dakota ranch."

South Dakota!

"Do you always handle accounts that far away, for a mere tutoring job?" Kathy voiced her thoughts.

"Ordinarily, no. Between us, as particular as this woman seemed to be, she might have already run through every agency between here and Rapid City. I remember her. She stopped in a few weeks ago when she was in the city for some kind of convention. At the time, I thought she seemed pleasant enough, but when she handed over her listing, I wondered if she might be tough to please. It's *very* definite. Would you care to hear the job description?"

"It couldn't hurt," Kathy replied.

Mr. Stockton read the listing in a monotone:

Widowed South Dakota rancher needs tutor to serve as a chaperon/companion to her fourteen-year-old daughter. Applicant must be intelligent, willing to work hard, and single, between the ages of twenty and twenty-five. Imperative applicant be physically attractive. Recent close-up photograph must accompany any inquiry. Experience in horseback-riding is helpful, but not necessary. Employer will furnish pleasant private quarters, all meals, and a generous salary based on qualifications and experience. Possibility of permanent position.

Kathy sat quietly considering the requirements. At twenty-four, she was just under the age limit. Mr. Stockton's eyes were questioning. However, brusque and exacting as the listing was, Kathy, too, wondered what the woman might be like.

"There is nothing to hold me in the St. Louis area," she mused. "I would be able to—"

"Oh-oh," Mr. Stockton's groan cut short her response. "I'm sorry. I overlooked something. This Mrs. Jarrett *insists* that any applicant must be a practicing Christian. I don't imagine you're . . . a *practicing* Christian."

16

"Yes, I am," Kathy said lightly, in the face of his rueful expression. "I 'practice' every day, and someday I hope to get it right."

Mr. Stockton's countenance brightened. "What do you think then? It's up to you."

"I'm interested."

Upon learning that Victoria Jarrett wanted only Christian applicants, Kathy felt reassured. The straightforward words reflected not a heartless dictator, but the candor of an individual who knew very definitely what she wanted and was unwilling to waste her time or that of a prospective employee with obscure language. Further, Kathy thought, the listing was a subtle warning that the Jarrett household operated on Christian principles with which unbelievers might feel uncomfortable.

"I'll make some inquiries then," Mr. Stockton said. "I'll try to reach her by telephone—to speed things up. That is, if Mrs. Jarrett will take my word that you're well-qualified and lovely to look at. Let me make some notes so I can describe you to her." He reached for a yellow notepad. Kathy felt her cheeks grow warm under his scrutiny as he scribbled, murmuring to himself: "Medium height. Good figure. Curly black hair. Eyes?" He squinted. "Blue. *Very* blue—you've beautiful eyes."

"Thank you."

He ripped off the page and tucked it into Kathy's folder. "I will need an address where you can be reached—and a telephone number."

Kathy supplied the name of the hotel where she and Trish were staying. "I can be reached through the switchboard," she said.

"Very well," Mr. Stockton said. "I'll be in touch with you. If this doesn't pan out—we'll try something else."

It was not Mr. Stockton who contacted her at the hotel the following morning. It was Victoria Jarrett herself! Her voice was a soft, gentle, Western drawl. Mrs. Jarrett introduced herself, expressed her pleasure with Kathy's credentials, and informed her that the job was hers.

17

"How soon do you want me?" Kathy countered, when Mrs. Jarrett asked how soon she could fly to South Dakota.

"How about the *day before yesterday*?"

Kathy chuckled, appreciating the knowledge that the woman was not without a sense of humor. "The day after tomorrow is probably more realistic."

"Good! I'll arrange for your flight and have a ticket waiting for you at the airport. Are there any questions?" she asked quickly.

"No. None," Kathy replied before she had had time to inventory her thoughts. But, by then, the connection was broken.

Why had Mrs. Jarrett said almost nothing about the young girl who would be Kathy's charge? She knew only that Margot Jarrett was fourteen and that she needed a tutor. Kathy couldn't help wondering if the mother was carefully avoiding further details for fear she would refuse the job!

"Quit jumping to conclusions," she berated herself.

Kathy sank to the occasional chair beside the desk where a Gideon Bible rested. She picked it up, wondering, as she had before, if she was one of the few inhabitants of the room to do so. Her own Bible—the leather soft, its pages like velvet from long use—had gone up in flames.

Kathy's heart soared, and she bowed her head in grateful thanksgiving. She had trusted Him and her needs had been provided. The job was evidence.

Kathy doodled on the hotel stationery, drawing up a list of items she would need to purchase. A must was an inexpensive suitcase. Then her thoughts wandered again.

Kathy had no idea what awaited her on the Black Diamond Ranch in the persons of Victoria Jarrett and her enigmatic daughter. She could only believe, so far at least, that her prayers had been answered and that her strong faith in God would continue to see her through.

CHAPTER 2

Two days later Trish, who planned to return to her parents' home in Kansas City in the hope of landing another teaching job by fall, saw Kathy off at Lambert Airport.

"This is the lightest I've traveled in my life," Kathy commented cheerfully as she checked her new suitcase containing a meager supply of clothing.

"One of the few good things to be said for losing everything you own in a fire," Trish grinned. "But that's my girl—always looking on the bright side. Say!" Trish's eyes narrowed with suspicion. "Are you sure your folks didn't really mean to name you *Pollyanna*?"

"Nut!" Kathy chuckled. "I'm sure going to miss you, Trish."

"I'm going to miss you, too, but I'm glad you're going. I have a feeling in my bones this is the right move for you. After all the time we put in together at Miss Atwood's, though, you're like family to me. And to mom and dad, too. You'll keep in touch? And promise you'll visit us when you get a chance?"

The public address system sounded above the hum of

conversation that buzzed throughout the terminal, announcing a departure.

"Let's go," Trish said. "That's your flight."

At the security station they faced each other and Kathy set down her cosmetics case long enough to give her good friend a solid hug.

"Things are going to work out for you," Trish murmured, her eyes glowing with hope.

Kathy smiled through a mist of tears. "Of course things will work out," she said with confidence. "Any Pollyanna worthy of the name knows that every dark cloud has a silver lining!"

When the final flight announcement was made, Kathy gave Trish another quick hug, then stepped in line to pass through the security stall.

"Good luck with your new job!" Trish called after her. She looked back in time to see Trish blowing a kiss. "And good luck in love!"

Trish's eyes were brimming with laughter until a severe, but playful frown swooped over her mischievous features. "One last word of warning. Don't fall in love with the first handsome cowboy you meet—and if you *do*—don't forget to write and tell me all about it!"

Laughing, Kathy was swept along in the throng of passengers streaming to the waiting aircraft. She boarded, handed her ticket to the flight attendant for verification, then took a window seat. Minutes later the attendant issued instructions. The aircraft taxied and lifted off. Kathy shifted in the plush seat to find a more comfortable position, then lost herself in thought.

In the past she'd laughed her way through Trish's "lectures" and "sermons" regarding her love life—or more accurately—her *lack* of one. Maybe Trish was right. Maybe she would meet some interesting people, including a tall, dark stranger. It was pleasant to contemplate.

The flight was uneventful. It seemed to Kathy she had only gotten settled in for the flight when it was over and the stewardess was giving instructions for landing.

Kathy buckled in and leaned back, finding it hard to absorb all the events of the past days. In a very few more minutes, someone would be meeting her, and she would be on her way to the Black Diamond Ranch in central South Dakota.

When the wheels of the jet touched the pavement, Kathy jolted softly with the impact, the braking action forcing her backward against the cushions.

Unfamiliar faces filled the observation area in the terminal. One by one the viewers moved away from the windows as they spotted a particular incoming passenger, and moved to the receiving area.

Scanning the crowd, Kathy could not find anyone who appeared to be looking for a slim, somewhat bewildered young woman. She decided to move to the baggage claim area, where she plucked her luggage from the revolving carousel. The crowd was thinning rapidly now. Suddenly all the stress and trauma of the past few days sent her head spinning, and she swayed dizzily.

At that moment a tall, ruggedly handsome man, jeaned and booted, stepped quickly to her side. "Hey! Are you all right?" he asked, taking in her pale face and steadying her with a firm grip.

The cowboy picked up the suitcase and led her to a plush seat. "Sit here a minute 'til you catch your breath." Consulting the slip of paper he extracted from his breast pocket, he said, "Since you're a perfect match for this description Mrs. J. gave me, you must be Katherine Newby." She nodded weakly. Not waiting for a reply, he continued, "Gosh, I'm not surprised you're tuckered out after all you've been through. Mrs. J. told me about the fire."

He paused, and Kathy assessed the voluble young man at her side. He was as tall as she remembered through the haze of her fainting spell. His coppery tan accentuated blond hair, streaked from shades of deep gold to pale platinum. He was looking at her with clear, hazel eyes.

"Guy Armitage, ma'am," he said, thrusting a large, lean hand in her direction. She took it gratefully. "I'm foreman of the Black Diamond Ranch. Guess I forgot my manners for a minute there when I saw you all weak and fainty. Sorry to be late.''

"I'm so glad to meet you, Mr. Armitage,'' Kathy smiled warmly, the color returning to her cheeks. "And no apology is needed. You're here now—that's what counts.''

"My name is Guy,'' he insisted. "Now let's get you on out to the Ranch. All it will take to fix you right up is some country sunshine and good, clean air.''

Guy reached for her luggage and held the door as they left the terminal.

"As many times as I've been to this airport lately, I should be able to drive it in my sleep. Wouldn't you know that the one time Mrs. J. wanted things to go without a hitch, there'd be a problem? The last time I got here an hour *early,* and the tutor's flight was an hour *late.*''

"The last time?" Kathy echoed weakly. She hoped her voice had not betrayed her growing uneasiness.

Guy laughed, with irony. "I picked her up a month ago yesterday, and brought her back three weeks ago today.''

In a very few words the attractive cowboy had spoken volumes. He squirmed uncomfortably. Another clue. Guy had obviously spoken hastily and now regretted his lack of foresight. She decided to press for some answers to the questions that had been plaguing her from the beginning.

"Mrs. Jarrett has employed several tutors lately, right?'' she probed.

Kathy could not read his thoughts, only the conflicting emotions playing over his features. She could not know that even in this short time, Guy had observed her closely— noting a resiliency of character, the lifted head and proud spirit of a thoroughbred. She did know, however, the moment he decided to level with her.

"Unfortunately that's true.'' He spoke after a long pause. "There was Miss Townsend. Margot couldn't stand her uppity ways. She expected Margot to behave like a 'proper' young lady at all times—wearing dresses and all.''

Kathy suppressed a giggle. Old Miss Atwood could have played that role to the hilt.

"Then there was Miss Brackney," Guy continued. "She ran into a rattlesnake one day and decided she preferred to take her chances with the muggers in New York City. Miss Bentley was the last—she and the Boss didn't hit it off." His expression was grim—an ominous sign.

Guy shifted his eyes to her face. "But don't let anything I say color your impression of the Ranch. Mrs. Jarrett has high hopes that at last she's found someone who will succeed where all the others have failed."

"But how could she possibly know that?" Kathy asked, perplexed. "The woman has never even laid eyes on me!"

"I guess it's enough to know that you share our beliefs and have faith to keep you going through the tough times," he said quietly.

Our beliefs, he had said. Guy—a Christian? Now Kathy knew why she had felt such instant rapport with him. It was like coming to the end of a long journey and meeting a stranger whose Best Friend was her Best Friend, too.

"I certainly hope I won't disappoint Mrs. Jarrett," Kathy fretted.

Guy's eyes crinkled at the corners, and he smiled as he smoothed a sandy moustache. "Somehow," he said, "I don't think you will."

Kathy matched her steps to Guy's long-legged stride as they crossed the lot to an aging station wagon. He stowed her luggage in the rear, then unlocked the car and helped her in.

"How long have you worked for Mrs. Jarrett?" she asked as they drove out of the parking lot.

"Ten years," he replied. "I met Jared Jarrett when I was attending the University of South Dakota. I wasn't able to finish college due to family circumstances, so I bummed the West for a couple of years, and rode the rodeo circuit. Broncs. Brahmas. Calf roping. I saw Jared again at the Belle Fourche rodeo, where I got hurt in the bull-riding competition. With no family and nowhere to go, I was

23

facing a real problem. To make a long story short, Jared insisted that I return to the Black Diamond to recuperate when I was released from the hospital. He wouldn't take no for an answer. I've been there ever since. A few years ago I was tempted to strike out on my own, but, with Jared gone . . . I couldn't leave Mrs. J.''

"She must be a remarkable woman to ranch alone.''

Guy smiled. "She's not really alone. Depending on the turnover, we have right at a dozen ranch hands year 'round. But, you're right. She *is* a remarkable woman.''

Kathy shifted on the car seat so she could see Guy's reaction to her next question.

"What about Margot Jarrett? When I spoke with her mother, she said very little about her. The call was completed before I could gather my wits enough to ask.''

Guy's jaw tensed at the mention of Margot, and in the following moments he seemed to carry on a mental debate. Kathy wasn't sure that this time he'd decide in favor of taking her into his confidence.

"Mrs. Jarrett might not want your impression of Margot affected by her personal feelings. Or mine,'' he pointed out.

"I understand that, Guy, but it's not fair to be kept in the dark. I'm afraid I'm already entertaining suspicions that might be far worse than the truth.''

Guy took a deep breath and began. "You win. Margot was four years old when I came to the Ranch. She was bright, friendly, sweet, and cute as a bug's ear. I've always liked little kids and Margot and I took a shine to each other. She used to be the happiest, most well-adjusted child you could hope for. Then she was in an airplane when it crashed on the Ranch. Her older sister, Jenny, was killed. Margot was in a coma for days. For about a month it was touch-and-go. She was so seriously injured that we all babied her for quite some time after she was released from the hospital.''

Kathy sat quietly, giving Guy time and space to tell his story without interruption.

"Margot wasn't well enough to return to school that year,

24

or study much at home. She fell behind and missed a grade. The next fall she went back to school, but it was hard for her. Kids who didn't know the situation accused her of having flunked a grade because she was older. Things like that hurt. Plus, she's terribly self-conscious about the few faint scars on her face. I don't think they're noticeable, but when she looks into a mirror, I think that's all she sees."

Kathy nodded sympathetically. Guy was loosening up. The more he reminisced about Margot, the more talkative he became.

"She was hurt—any kid would've been—by the cutting remarks at school. Her grades slipped drastically. Mrs. J. tried to comfort her, but it was like Margot didn't believe a word her mother told her, or resented her. She began shutting everyone out, including me," Guy sighed in frustration.

Only then did Kathy comment. "She must be an unhappy girl. Confused. Angry."

Guy nodded. "Yep, she is to be pitied in many ways. She's had a lot to swallow. Her dad was killed in a freak accident on horseback. She was injured in the crash and lost her sister. The problems at school . . ." Guy paused.

"Last year Margot masterminded one fiasco after another 'til she was kicked out at mid-term. The school board refuses to let her reenroll unless she shows a definite improvement in attitude. Margot's determined not to change. More than anything she wants to go away to school this fall."

"Where?" Kathy asked.

Guy's smile was sardonic. "Anywhere, Kathy, so long as it's far away from the Black Diamond. Her mother, of course, doesn't want that. She knows that a girl Margot's age needs someone to care about her, to keep her in line, and at the same time, to set a good example . . . whether she accepts it or not."

"Mrs. Jarrett has her hands full," Kathy murmured.

"You're her last hope. Not one of the tutors Mrs. J. has tried during these past months has been a committed Christian. And Mrs. Jarrett hopes that Margot may respond to someone nearer her own age."

"I'll do my best," Kathy took a deep breath.

"We're all going to be praying that you do," Guy said. "Now, I don't mean to change the subject," he said abruptly, "but I thought you might like to know something about the area we're passing through."

Kathy was enthralled by the stark barrenness of the land, the fantastic formations of rock, rugged terrain, and fearsome environment of the famous South Dakota Badlands. Jagged peaks of rock jutted into the clear, indigo sky to form natural turrets, spires, and majestic towers that soared as high as the craggy canyons cut deep. A labyrinth of valleys tangled and twined for miles. The rocks seemed to be changing constantly, shifting in patterns and colors, like a kaleidoscope. The landscape, magnificent in its vast expanse was, nevertheless, hauntingly lonely and inhospitable. Kathy shivered.

"The formations were caused by erosion," Guy was saying. "The rock here is soft and unconsolidated—it wears away easily. In this part of the state we have some real gullywashers—followed by scorching droughts."

Guy explained that when the torrents of rain water slashed the soft rocks, the swirling currents wore away the grainy composition of the rock, leaving creations molded by nature's savage inspiration.

"It took the force of water many centuries to carve out what we're seeing now."

Kathy contrasted the fierce scene with the serenity of the Illinois farmscapes—fields of soybeans and corn, dotted with clumps of trees—oak, maple, hickory, and locust. And she thought of the early settlers who faced this formidable terrain. Would they have regretted bypassing the rich farmland in the "East River" section of South Dakota only to forge ahead, past the Missouri River and the Missouri Breaks, delving deeper into the "West River" region until they came face to face with the Badlands, as brutal and barbaric then as now?

"It really *is* bad land."

"But other states can't hold a candle to what we have here in South Dakota," Guy said. "These are thought to be the most rugged and picturesque formations of their type in the world."

"I still feel sorry for the poor settlers who faced them in covered wagons. It must've been cruelly disheartening to travel so far only to be stopped by this."

Guy nodded agreement. "I'm sure it sent many of the less hardy settlers on long detours around the area in the trek West, or else it discouraged them so roundly they scurried back to farm in the East River section."

Viewed from the valley of the master stream, Guy explained, the fringe of the Badlands would rise jaggedly against the horizon like a saw-toothed mountain range. But if you approached from the uplands there was no hint of what lay ahead until some brave traveler reached the ravine and discovered the intricate maze beyond. Kathy shuddered involuntarily.

She was not disappointed to leave the Badlands, and the remainder of the trip through the West River section went quickly.

"We're not far from the Ranch now," Guy said as he turned off the main highway. "Up ahead at the fenceline is the boundary of the Jarrett spread. That's the wild horse pasture."

High barbed-wire fences, tautly strung, separated the pasture from the roadside. The pasture was rough and rugged; the grass, lush and green. Tangled thickets, brush-lined gullies, and ravines cut along sloping hills.

"*Wild* horses?" Kathy thought wild horses had become extinct along with the gunslingers, hangings, and train holdups of the Old West.

"Wild," Guy reaffirmed. "The mustangs are raised as a cash crop at the Ranch. We sell off a crop of horses every year."

Kathy was fascinated when Guy told her about the business of raising wild broncos, horses that would be sold at

27

auction sales to rodeo contractors. These men owned strings of wild horses that they furnished, for a fee, to towns sponsoring rodeos.

"The auction sales are like a rodeo. Before the broncos are sold, prospective buyers want to see them in action. Mr. Jarrett was killed riding one of the buckers at a sale. The Jarretts used to ride their own horses—with the help of the ranch hands. But after Mr. J. was killed, Mrs. Jarrett put a stop to that. He died in her arms before the ambulance could get him to the hospital."

"How tragic!" Kathy exclaimed. "I'm surprised she didn't get rid of the horses."

"Never," Guy said softly. "The wild horses are as much a part of the Black Diamond as the Jarretts themselves.

"The first pair of mustangs—a filly and colt—were brought to the Black Diamond from Wyoming, by Jared's great-grandfather. Mrs. J. insists that if the mustangs must be ridden for the contractors' approval during the selling, then only hired riders—experts who ride for a price—will be used. She won't have any of her hands risking life and limb to save her a few dollars." Guy slowed and turned the station wagon onto a long, winding lane. "You can see the headquarters when we top the next rise."

Kathy was surprised—shaken—when Guy crested the knoll and she beheld the Black Diamond Ranch for the first time. She had expected to find a small place, a modest home, a few stables, several corrals, a bunkhouse for the hands.

There were so many large buildings the ranch headquarters resembled a small village. The beautiful two-story home of Bedford stone crowned the hill. The bunkhouse, though modest by comparison, was more elaborate than many residences in suburban St. Louis. The stables were large and freshly painted. Corrals, fences, pastures, and crop land divided the spread for as far as Kathy could see from her vantage point, laid out before her like a multicolored patchwork quilt.

"Impressive, isn't it?" Guy spoke.

28

"That's hardly the word for it. I never dreamed it would be like this. From what I knew of Mrs. Jarrett I assumed she was a widow working a ranch, barely able to make ends meet."

Guy roared at the idea. He rested his hand over Kathy's for a fleeting moment and gave it a comforting squeeze.

"May I give you a piece of very good, well-intentioned advice—as a friend?"

"Please do," she invited.

Guy's hazel eyes crinkled at the corners. "Don't ever *assume* anything about any of the Jarretts. None of them."

Guy parked between a late-model Lincoln Continental and a Jaguar. An assortment of pickups and jeeps was parked near the stables, and several older model cars, in front of the bunkhouse. Kathy wondered if everything she'd assumed about Mrs. Jarrett and her ranch would be as quickly shattered as her ideas about their lifestyle. Guy correctly interpreted her expression.

"Don't worry. Mrs. Jarrett doesn't put on airs. She'd be the same if she didn't have two nickels to rub together. She's going to love you, Kathy, and you can't help adoring her. We all do."

When they got out of the station wagon, the couple heard the idling engine of a low-slung sportscar.

"Jared's back," Guy stated matter-of-factly.

"*Jared?*" Kathy faced Guy, mystified.

"Jared Jarrett—Mrs. Jarrett's oldest and only son—heir to the Black Diamond fortune."

"I thought he was *dead!*" Kathy gasped. "I thought you said. . ."

Guy seemed amused. "Jared is very much alive, as you will find out for yourself soon enough. I warned you not to assume anything about the family. That goes double for Jared."

Kathy didn't comment as Guy filled her in on the man of the Jarrett household, and led her up a curving walk past a lily pond, bordered by fragrant flowers.

When Kathy and Guy reached the house, the wide double

doors shot open, almost knocking them over. Jared Jarrett rushed past, glaring down at the typed papers in his hand. Menacing dark brows formed a deep *V* over gun-metal gray eyes. When he glanced up, his gaze swept Kathy indifferently. Then his eyes returned to her face, lingering there for a long moment.

Guy dropped her suitcase with a thud, took Kathy firmly by the elbow, and stepped forward. "Boss, this is Katherine Newby—Margot's new tutor."

Boss! Kathy thought with alarm as she extended her hand. *This* was "the Boss" who did not always "hit it off" with tutors whom he found reason to dismiss.

"I—I've heard a great deal about you, Mr. Jarrett," she stammered miserably.

"My pleasure," he mouthed, but it was evident that this meeting was anything but a pleasure. The amenities behind them, Mr. Jarrett turned his attention to his foreman, with whom he hurriedly discussed some pressing matter of business. Kathy was chilled by his icy indifference. Apparently Mr. Jarrett figured she'd last no longer than any of the rest. Therefore, it wasn't worth his while to bother learning her name.

Despite his brusque manner, Kathy couldn't take her eyes off him. Jared Jarrett was a handsome man—one of the most attractive she had ever seen. He was tall—taller than Guy—which meant the Boss of the Black Diamond stood well over six feet. Her head would barely reach his shoulder, she thought, blushing. Lean and broad-shouldered, he looked like a Hollywood actor playing cowboy, in his expensively tailored Western suit. But Jared Jarrett was the real thing!

His interesting face was bronzed from the sun, and a deep cleft in his firm chin suggested both strength and implacability. Thick, gently waving hair, black as a raven's wing, was in slight disarray, as though he had just run his hands through it in a moment of exasperation. One stray lock fell irresistibly over his forehead. For an instant, Kathy was compelled to reach up and smooth it back—as she would for a small boy in distress. But the impenetrable gray eyes stopped her.

When Jared turned away and strode to the waiting Jaguar, she felt a strange sense of loss. Guy gave her a searching look.

"Now that you've met the Beast of the Black Diamond, how about meeting the Beauty?"

Before Kathy could respond, the front door opened for the second time. A serene woman stepped outside. Her white hair was beautifully coiffed, and her sparkling eyes were a clear, warm topaz, flecked with brown. By the cut of her perfectly tailored tan pantsuit, Kathy knew it was expensive. The woman took Kathy's hand in both of hers. Her smile was as welcoming as her words. Jared Jarrett had made Kathy feel like an intruder. Victoria Jarrett greeted her as if she were a member of the family returning home after a long absence.

Guy took Kathy's luggage to her quarters, leaving the two women to get acquainted in the foyer. Within a matter of minutes, Kathy knew that Victoria Jarrett was a person worth knowing—loving and compassionate, but strong and resolute. She would be more than an employer. She would be a friend.

Even though circumstances and personalities were not at all what Kathy had expected to find, her sense of adventure was aroused. There was a decided dark side to the Black Diamond—but the treasures to be mined here were infinitely worth the risk.

CHAPTER 3

"I COULD TAKE YOU right to your quarters if you're tired from the trip, Katherine," Mrs. Jarrett was saying. "Or, if you prefer, I could show you around now. Perhaps there would be time for a private chat. There's so much I want to know about you, dear, and to share with you . . ."

"I'm not tired at all! And please call me 'Kathy,'" she protested, revived by the excitement of her new surroundings. "I'd love to see the place! And Guy has already given me a brief history and geography lesson of the state."

"That Guy," Mrs. Jarrett shook her head fondly. "I don't know what we'd do without him around here. Now, let's start our tour with the ell, which houses all the offices where we conduct business."

Kathy followed the lithe woman down a long, wood-paneled hallway that exited from the foyer before opening into the living room and family quarters.

"My office is on the right," she pointed out. "Jared's is the larger one on the end. And we have prepared a suite for you directly across from mine."

Mrs. Jarrett opened the door to her office. The draperies were pulled back, framing a scene that rivaled the subdued country paintings of one of the Old Masters. Exquisitely groomed horses grazed in the lush green pasture.

"Those horses are my pets," Mrs. Jarrett said lightly. "They're Blue Star Arabians. Most of them are desert-bred, and a few respond only to commands in Arabic."

Kathy admired the beautifully proportioned animals, ranging in hue from a milk white to rich brown—all of them with the "teacup" noses for which the breed is noted, noses so dainty that the horses are said to be able to drink from a teacup.

"The trophies are for the Blue Stars?" she asked, noting a large, glass trophy case filled with gleaming awards.

"Yes. But I'm not as active with the breed as I used to be. Over the years, I had my Blue Stars, and Tom had his broncos," Mrs. Jarrett sighed.

"Your office is lovely," Kathy remarked, changing what she felt might be a painful subject.

The room was tastefully decorated. Green plants thrived in lush profusion, giving the room a cozy atmosphere. The furnishings were feminine, yet comfortable, in rich leathers of soft earth tones with russet and dark green accents. The room suited Mrs. Jarrett perfectly.

"I love it! And I'm hoping you will like yours equally well. Let's go take a look."

Kathy's office was surprisingly large. The carpet, a deep Aztec gold, richly contrasted with pecan paneling. A built-in bookcase covered one wall from floor to ceiling, and a desk was constructed to adjoin at the corner. Full-length drapes were drawn over a window that almost filled another wall. When Mrs. Jarrett drew the drapes, a spectacular view of beautifully manicured lawns and flowerbeds spread before them.

To one side, almost a separate room, was a small sitting area composed of several occasional chairs, reading lamps, and a low coffee table. Artfully arranged to blend with the decor were filing cabinets and a bookcase that held a set of encyclopedias and a large, unabridged dictionary.

"You do like it!" Mrs. Jarrett exclaimed with delight.

"It's perfect!" Kathy said, smiling her approval.

"This is where you'll be tutoring Margot. Since she'll be freshest and most rested in the morning, you'll probably want to work with her then, although I'll give you free rein in planning your regimen."

"Mornings are usually best," she agreed.

"Your afternoons will be your own, as will your evenings, although . . . I would appreciate it very much if you would be available to my daughter any time she needs your companionship."

The hollow ring in Mrs. Jarrett's voice indicated that she dared not hope Margot would seek out her new tutor. Even as she smiled, a dark shadow crossed Mrs. Jarrett's amber eyes and she fingered her necklace nervously.

"I'd be pleased to spend as much time with Margot as you like," Kathy assured her.

"Or as she will permit," Mrs. Jarrett corrected. "But I do want you to be sure to reserve some time for yourself each day. There are many things to occupy you during your leisure time. Books on the shelves. The swimming pool out back. Croquet set up nearby. And there are horses if you wish to ride. If you want to go to town, a car is always available." Her warm smile underscored the sincerity of her offer.

"What more could anyone possibly need or want?" Kathy marveled.

"It does seem we have everything here," Mrs. Jarrett replied, her voice strained. "But I find that I must be away on business quite frequently." When her gaze met Kathy's, she seemed to be pleading for understanding. "That's why it is imperative that, in my absence, Margot have someone she can . . . relate to."

Kathy nodded. She had noticed the calendar blotter on Mrs. Jarrett's desk when they were in her office. It had been heavily penciled with engagements and appointments.

"Although I'm not as active in the Blue Star Association as I was when I held an office in that organization, I'm still involved with it and travel on horse business. I'm kept far

35

busier, however, by charitable organizations and mission fund-raising drives."

Kathy nodded understandingly, then smiled. "Everyone must appreciate what you do. These groups certainly need you."

"Yes," Mrs. Jarrett said quietly. "They *do* need me, and that's why I want to be available to them."

Although Mrs. Jarrett said no more Kathy caught the glint of pain that flickered in her gentle eyes, and she knew that the lovely older woman lived tirelessly for the various charities and missions because they needed her in a way, Kathy suspected, that her family had let her know they did *not!*

"If you've seen enough of your office, I'll show you the rest of the house. You must meet the wonderful woman who keeps things running smoothly here—my housekeeper, cook, and best friend, Mrs. Otis."

"I'd love to meet her," Kathy smiled.

"I warn you that Oatie is going to view you as a challenge. As slim as you are, Kathy, don't be surprised if Oatie doesn't seem instantly inspired to fatten you up."

Kathy laughed softly. "That shouldn't be much of a challenge—I'm a pushover for good cooking."

Mrs. Jarrett halted in the long living room. A fieldstone fireplace and large hearth, with built-in bookshelves on both sides, dominated the far end of the room. Rustic, wooden beams, stained dark, with ship-lapped lighter planking created the ceiling. A wagon-wheel chandelier hung over a heavy, wooden coffee table positioned on a bright Indian rug, one of many that accented the terra-cotta floor. Heavy, rich leather and wood sofas, chairs, and ottomans, flanked by reading lamps, were situated throughout the room. It was a room that begged one to curl up before the fire with a good book.

Mrs. Jarrett passed an open archway that led into a massive dining room.

"Dinner is a formal affair when we have company. Tom was active in state politics, and it wasn't unusual to have this room filled with guests. Now we often eat in the dining hall with the ranch hands.''

Kathy sensed that Mrs. Jarrett very much missed those happy days.

''And here we are in Oatie's domain,'' she said, and led the way into the large, cheery kitchen with gingham wallpaper, rows of cabinets, lots of counter space, and the most modern of appliances.

At the sound of Mrs. Jarrett's voice, a plump woman in a flowered housedress, wearing comfortable shoes on her feet and a beaming smile on her broad, ruddy face, turned from the batter she was stirring. A red apron was tied around her ample waist. Her brown eyes snapped with humor, and a thick brown knot of hair rested at the nape of her neck.

''Mrs. Otis—this is Kathy Newby—Margot's new tutor.''

Kathy extended her hand. Mrs. Otis laid down her wooden spoon, wiped her hands on the hem of her apron, and gave Kathy a warm smile before she frowned, clucking.

''Before you leave here,'' Oatie warned, ''I'll put some meat on those bones of yours, honey.''

Mrs. Jarrett winked at Kathy. ''See! What did I tell you? Oatie's incorrigible!''

Kathy smiled, trying to refuse as Mrs. Otis held out a huge ceramic cookie jar. ''Fresh-baked this afternoon,'' Oatie tempted. ''With lots of chocolate chips.''

''I'd love to, but I don't want to spoil my appetite.''

She took one of the buttery cookies, but refused another.

''That reminds me! I almost forgot,'' Mrs. Otis said. ''Jared called a short while ago and told me he was bringing a guest home for dinner.''

''Did he say who?'' his mother asked.

''Yes . . . Alana,'' the cook said carefully. ''Jared said he had gone to fetch Margot from town and that Alana decided to join them for the evening.''

''Very well,'' Mrs. Jarrett said. For some reason, her voice seemed to grow weary. But when the lovely woman faced Kathy, her smile gave away none of her feelings.

"Then dress for dinner tonight will be formal."

Mrs. Jarrett led the way to the curving staircase which ascended to an open hallway. It skirted the bedrooms and looked down on the living room, separated only by a heavy wooden railing.

"Perhaps I should eat in the kitchen with Oatie, or with the hands," Kathy suggested ruefully. "I'm not sure I have anything appropriate to wear."

"Nonsense!" Mrs. Jarrett responded. "I won't hear of it. I know you lost almost everything in the fire. The dress you have on now is perfectly acceptable." Her tone indicated the matter was settled. "This room," she said, "Is Jared's—though he seldom uses it. He has a cot in his office," she explained further, "and an adjoining dressing room. This next one is Margot's." She opened the third door. "And this will be your room. It was Jenetia's."

The room was done in a soft, buttery yellow and white. The furniture, white wicker, was airily feminine. Above the wainscoting, a delicate yellow-and-white floral paper covered the walls. The adjoining bath maintained the color scheme.

"It's lovely!" Kathy exclaimed. "It's the kind of decor a girl dreams about."

"My girl *did* dream about it," Mrs. Jarrett said, her voice softened by long-ago memories. "When we decided to build a new home, this is what Jenny wanted. She was an amazing girl, Kathy. You'd have liked our Jenny very much. We still miss her. At least . . . Jared and I do."

Mrs. Jarrett seemed eager to talk further but decided against it. She consulted her slim, gold wristwatch, and quickly made excuses.

"I've a few things to do. We'll eat at seven. I'll see you then. You'll be meeting Margot . . . and Alana."

Kathy had the uneasy feeling that Mrs. Jarrett had just issued a warning.

When she heard voices in the living room below, she knew dinner would be served shortly. Casting an anxious glance at the full-length mirror, Kathy decided she looked presentable in a simple pink summer frock. She wore no accent jewelry. She brushed her curly black hair until it shone and applied a light touch of lip gloss to her gently curved mouth.

She was halfway down the long staircase before she realized she was overhearing a heated family discussion—certainly not intended for the ears of a guest!

"Margot! You had no right to charge that ridiculous-looking dress to my account!" stormed Jared.

"But Alana picked it out for me . . ." The younger girl looked to the willowy redhead for support. "You always said you liked her style." Margot's voice was petulant, whining.

"That's not the point!" he persisted. "You are never to charge against my account *without my permission!* Is that clear?"

The girl raised her hands to her face, sniffling. "You would never have been so mean to Jenny. Miss Perfect could do no wrong . . ."

"Margot, dear," interjected Mrs. Jarrett, "I hardly think that Jenny is the subject here . . ."

Catching a brilliant gleam from Margot's hand, Jared grabbed her wrist. "And *what* do you think you are doing with the Jarrett ring?"

The small party gasped in unison as he tore the ring from her hand and held it in his palm—a magnificent sapphire set in platinum and surrounded with perfectly matched diamonds.

"I was just trying it on with the dress . . ." Margot's voice trailed away as she caught sight of Kathy standing on the stairway—frozen in horror. She blushed deeply as all eyes turned to observe her awkward entrance. Mrs. Jarrett, with dignity and grace, crossed the room and took her hand, gathering her into the group.

"This is Katherine Newby, Margot's new tutor." The woman spoke with perfect composure, as if the ugly little scene had never taken place.

"Kathy, you and Jared have met, I believe."

39

"We've met," he said flatly.

"This is Jared's . . . friend," Mrs. Jarrett hesitated only briefly. "Alana Fontaine—Katherine Newby."

The two young women assessed each other. Kathy was struck with the ivory perfection of the flaming-haired beauty, who had stepped to Jared's side and was holding his arm in a proprietary manner. The two made a striking couple, she thought.

Alana's green gaze, catlike, measured the other girl, missing no detail of her simple frock or the open, friendly expression. Though Alana's full mouth curved into a generous smile, her eyes remained cool. The new tutor was pretty—prettier than most of the others. Unlike them, however, this one did nothing to enhance her good figure or her best features. Alana's smile widened. No competition here, she decided. A passionate man like Jared Jarrett would not give such a demure girl a second glance!

"We've been looking forward to meeting you, Kathy," the curvaceous beauty purred. Expensive gold bracelets jangled from Alana's slim wrist as she took the other girl's hand, then dropped it quickly to fling a lock of coppery hair from her face.

Though Alana's smile was warm, Kathy shuddered. Even as the beautiful girl predicted their friendship, Kathy felt no instant rapport as she had with Guy. She sensed that, in spite of Alana's words, the girl didn't like her.

Mrs. Jarrett's grip on Kathy's arm tensed. They turned to face Margot who had grown bored with the introductions and the stir she had caused by returning to the Ranch wearing the sophisticated dress Alana had helped her select.

"Margot, this is your new tutor, Miss Newby. Kathy —my youngest child."

Margot glared.

"I—uh—have been eager to meet you, Margot," Kathy faltered. The words of greeting died on her lips.

"So." Margot regarded her with an amused air. "You're the new slave-driver, huh, Kathy?" She spoke softly, her tone husky, a careful imitation of Alana's seductive voice.

So that was it! When she caught Margot's quick glance at Alana, Kathy understood. The defiant young girl was trying to impress the older one. Margot and Alana Fontaine had perhaps already placed bets on how long *this* silly tutor would last at the Black Diamond Ranch.

"It's *Miss Newby* to you, Margot," Mrs. Jarrett corrected.

Margot gave her mother an impertinent look and tossed her long ash-blonde hair impatiently. Mrs. Jarrett fingered her necklace, a move not unnoticed by Margot, who delighted in the fact she could upset her mother any time she chose.

Kathy spoke up. "Why not?" she asked. "My friends call me 'Kathy.' I would be pleased if you would, too, Margot."

Her attempt at finding a chink in the girl's armor failed. Margot was no fool. She could see what Kathy was trying to do, and cooperation was the last thing she would offer.

"Dinner is served," Mrs. Otis announced, defusing the inflammatory atmosphere.

Oatie stepped into the living room, beaming at Kathy. There was no missing the distrust in Oatie's eyes when she regarded Alana, who treated Oatie as if she were a servant, and not a cherished member of the Jarrett household.

Kathy studied the faces across from her at the table—a sullen Margot; Alana, her finely chiseled features masking all emotion; Jared, still scowling darkly, taking his place at the head. The air was highly charged, and Kathy found herself wishing she had insisted on eating a bite with Oatie in the kitchen or even with Guy and the other ranch hands, where good-natured banter would have made dining a pleasure.

She jumped when Mrs. Jarrett touched her hand beneath the snowy linen tablecloth and suggested that she ask the blessing.

Kathy bowed her head and prayed simply: "Thank You, Lord, for good food, for new friends . . . and give us the courage to meet the challenges before us. Amen."

Kathy raised her head in time to see Alana and Margot exchange amused glances. Their eyes were mocking—not so much of her, Kathy felt—but of the faith she proclaimed openly. The realization hurt more than if *she* had been the target of their ridicule.

Dinner was a wretched affair. Alana Fontaine was an expert in ambiguities. Throughout the meal she succeeded in taking cruel jabs at Kathy, while appearing to the others as though she were genuinely interested in the newcomer's family, her education, her background.

Jared was silent. He looked at Kathy only when it was necessary to pass her a dish, and seemed oblivious to her discomfort under the lash of Alana's sarcastic tongue. Or, if he were aware of her mental anguish, the glowering glances he occasionally bestowed on Kathy indicated clearly that he considered *her* the cause of the tension at the Jarrett table . . . not Alana!

When Oatie removed the sherbet dishes, Kathy was at last relieved to fold her napkin and escape the third-degree grilling under the guise of friendly interest. No one lingered over a second cup of coffee.

Jared, his features contorted with anger, ushered Alana to his Jaguar. They departed as soon as the girl had called out her glib good-byes. Margot scurried to her room before her mother could take her to task about the dress she had charged—and the borrowed ring. And even Mrs. Jarrett, obviously distraught, slipped away to her own quarters at the earliest opportunity.

Finding herself alone, Kathy entered the kitchen to chat with Oatie, while the cook cleaned up after the evening meal.

"Please let me help."

"Help? No need to. I can handle the kitchen by myself." It was true. The plump cook was happiest in her domain, doing what she loved most—feeding hungry people. "I don't need the help, dearie, but I'd love a bit of company," Oatie admitted as she filled the dishwasher. "I couldn't help overhearing . . ."

She glanced uneasily at the louvered doors that kept the kitchen out of sight of the dining room, but passed conversation with ease. "Alana made it tough on you tonight, didn't she?"

"Yes," Kathy sighed, then added, "but that's to be expected when you're dining with strangers for the first time. After you get past the awkward stage and can become friends . . ."

"Hmph!" sniffed Oatie, cutting her short. "Don't toy with the idea that Alana Fontaine will ever be your friend—no matter what she says!"

It was as obvious to Oatie as it was to Kathy that "Miss Newby," her excellent qualifications notwithstanding, would last no longer than had any of the others . . .

Alana and Margot would see to that!

CHAPTER 4

"I'M GOING TO MY ROOM to get ready for bed and watch a bit of television before I turn in, lovey," Mrs. Otis said when she snapped out the kitchen light. "Morning comes early for these old bones. I have to get the ranch hands fed by dawn."

"I'll see you at breakfast then," Kathy said. "Good night, Oatie."

"Good night to you," Mrs. Otis answered as she shuffled to her quarters not far from the kitchen.

Kathy had no desire to return to her own room just yet. But she didn't want the company of Mrs. Jarrett, who was in her office, nor of Margot who sat in the living room, staring pointedly at the television set when Kathy passed through the room.

The night air was cool, the velvet darkness inviting when she stepped outside and closed the heavy front door behind her. She wanted—*needed*—to be alone.

Kathy seated herself on an ornate, wrought-iron chair positioned near the end of the porch. She took a deep breath, savoring the sharp, pungent pine scent of the ever-green shrubs, and closed her eyes reflecting on the events of the day. It seemed almost a lifetime, instead of only a few short hours since Trish had seen her off at the airport and since she had arrived at the Black Diamond with Guy.

She thought of the people who composed the intricate pieces of the family puzzle—their individualistic traits striking fire like flint as they crossed paths. Some of them—Guy, Oatie, and Mrs. Jarrett—had become instant friends. That was a comfort. But she would have to learn to love Margot, the little rebel who had erected an almost impenetrable shield around herself. Alana, she feared, would never want to be close—to anyone but Jared. *Jared!* At the thought of the handsome Boss of the Black Diamond, her pulse quickened.

The moment of their first meeting was branded deep into her memory. The look in his gray eyes when they had briefly met her own gaze had been almost welcoming, flashing with surprised recognition. And something else—not unlike admiration—was reflected there. But only for a moment. Then he had hardened his expression until his eyes became gray granite. It was almost as if Jared thought he knew her and was trying to recall where they had met, only to decide an instant later that he had made a mistake.

Later, she wondered if Jared Jarrett had been as attracted to her—even momentarily—as she was to him. At dinner that evening, with Jared's attention riveted on Alana, Kathy dismissed the idea as absurd. In fact, as the evening progressed, she had seemed to be the source of Jared's increasing irritation.

Jared Jarrett, the Boss of the Black Diamond, was her employer. She was a fool to hope he'd ever be anything else. She'd been a fool to think he'd pay her a moment's notice when he could have his pick of women, and had already chosen a beauty like Alana Fontaine.

"You're a fool!"

The harsh words broke the still night to echo Kathy's thoughts. Startled, she whirled and searched the darkness for the source, even as she recognized Jared's voice.

Kathy had no idea that Jared had returned to the Ranch,

or that, when she had slipped outdoors for a few moments of solitude and fresh air before retiring to her quarters, she had drifted to the very spot where Jared often spent his private moments.

There he stood, lighting a cigarette. She hadn't felt so tongue-tied since she was Margot's age. Ignoring her silence, Jared crossed the short distance between them with a grace unusual in such a large man.

"Miss Newby," he barked, "you're a fool!"

Kathy felt violated by his presence, hurt by his rudeness. Willing herself not to cry, even as the hot tears burned behind her eyes, she smiled up into his face.

"Why, Mr. Jarrett . . . to what do I owe this unprofessional analysis?" she asked.

"You miss my point. Dinner was a disaster because you acted the part of a spineless fool." Jared's voice hardened. He looked away from Kathy as if she hurt his eyes and stared out into the darkness before turning back indignantly.

"You probably earned a few points with mother—but you lost as many with me! *She* would approve of your Christian performance and turn-the-other-cheek routine. The only thing that impressed me about your behavior tonight was your ability to turn the other cheek so many times without suffering a whiplash injury!"

"What's the matter with you? Why didn't you give Alana a taste of her own medicine? She was a positive cat tonight, and you took it all without so much as a whimper. Don't you have any self-respect? You'd have had every right to tell both of them—Alana and Margot—to shut their nasty mouths and no one would have blamed you a bit. I kept waiting for you to put a stop to it, and you could have and should have!"

Kathy was surprised by the vehemence in his voice, and at the same time wondered what kind of relationship he had with the fiery red-haired beauty if he could desire to see her humiliated by another woman.

When he finally paused to take another drag on his cigarette, Kathy spoke.

47

"I probably could have won your respect with that kind of behavior instead of earning your contempt, but I don't care what you think of me. And, instead of feeling hurt, since our values are so different, maybe I should consider it a compliment to be labeled a fool by your standards!"

Jared winced, then smiled boyishly, the grin making his dark features more handsome. His eyes softened with amusement.

"Touché," he conceded softly. The scorn left his voice, to be replaced by a kinder tone. "You're right, of course, about that. But it doesn't mean that I enjoyed watching you take a raking. I expected that eventually you'd speak up and end Alana's harassment once and for all. You sure had openings enough. I was disappointed when you didn't take them."

"I could have found a lot of openings, I suppose," she admitted. "But I wasn't going to set aside my own principles to even the score. Not only would I have betrayed myself and my beliefs, but I'd have set a very poor example for Margot. Two wrongs don't make a right, you know, and it's a good thing for you I don't believe that. Since you just called me a fool several times, I am entitled to a few choice words which I will refrain from using."

"You state your philosophies well . . ."

"Not mine," Kathy corrected. "That's just one of the principles all Christian people live by. It wasn't my idea—it was His."

"What is it about you people?" he muttered under his breath.

But Jared knew what she meant. He turned away, sensing a Presence within her, a greater power that gave Kathy Newby strength even when she was outnumbered. When Kathy looked up at him, her innocent face lovely in the pale moonlight, Jared Jarrett felt lost, uncertain. Emotions, strong and conflicting, raged within him. He was desperately aware of a need to escape her, just as he was helplessly drawn to her, and all she represented.

Kathy turned to enter the house. Jared touched her arm,

stopping her. Her gaze was questioning. Jared found it difficult to speak. His words were as soft as the breeze that rippled the leaves on the trees overhead.

"I want to apologize," he murmured.

Kathy smiled, and he knew he was instantly, totally forgiven his outburst.

"I called you a fool, Kathy, but I was the one who was a fool not to realize that Margot needs you."

Jared seemed about to say more, then changed his mind, and he stared after Kathy as she stepped toward the house, hurrying, not trusting herself to stay a moment longer.

"Good night, Jared," she whispered, then she was gone.

Margot did need the influence of a woman like Kathy Newby, Jared mused. Even so, he was not sure that Kathy's presence at the Black Diamond would be good for him. Already, she had turned his thoughts upside down. And he wasn't the only one touched by her innocent beauty. Jared had seen the look of admiration on Guy's face. This tutor *was* decidedly different from all the others.

As he studied the starry South Dakota sky, Jared Jarrett fervently hoped that, in her attempts to put Margot's young life back together, she wouldn't tear his own apart.

Since the moment they met, he had been like a man possessed. In the moments when he wanted to protect Kathy from hurt, he railed at her, troubling her further. When he most wanted to escape from her, he was helplessly drawn to her. When he needed his old confidence, the thought of Kathy filled him with new, and unpleasant, uncertainty. With a glance, she could make him doubt his values, and wonder about everything he had chosen to believe.

Jared's memories spanned the last years, touching on the high points, skimming over the low. All in all, he had carved out a good life—a life he liked and one that suited him. It was his policy to live hard and fast, making quick decisions both in business and in personal affairs, living with the outcome, right or wrong, answering to no one but himself.

This small girl, who seemed very much unaware of the influence she was exerting on the entire household—even on Alana—seemed capable of unsettling Jared's comfortable existence. He knew that in order to preserve the life he enjoyed, he'd have to heed the small voice that warned him to avoid her.

"There's one sure way to stop that," Jared spoke aloud. His firm voice took on quiet determination, and he arose and went into the ranch office, locking his office door behind him, as if that action would be sufficient to bar the disturbing girl from his thoughts. "I'll stay out of her way," he vowed softly, "and concentrate on my work until I forget all about her."

With fresh resolve, Jared took his place at his desk and reached for a pile of papers awaiting his attention. He leaned back in his chair, and rested his booted feet on the scarred corner of his mahogany desk.

His gaze fell on Alana's smiling picture, and lingered there as a solution formed in his mind. He would put Katherine Newby out of his mind.

"With Alana's help," he murmured, as he studied the beautiful picture. Any attraction Kathy offered would pale in the face of Alana's tempting suggestions.

The next morning Kathy was in her office early to prepare for Margot's arrival. There was time to review the lesson material and to pray for direction as she dealt with the difficult girl.

During her four years at Miss Atwood's Academy, she had successfully handled some tough numbers. Some of the girls had been expelled from the public school system as incorrigibles. They were angry, resentful, and incendiary —ready to erupt over the most trivial thing. Some of them had reason to be belligerent and were to be pitied for the burdens they shouldered alone. Most of them, like Margot, labored under additional problems of their own making. Gradually, with a lot of prayer and persistence, Kathy had managed to break through the crusty exteriors of most of the girls, to touch the sensitive, inner persons who were screaming silently for help. Though Margot was a challenge, these experiences gave Kathy solid hope that she would not always be indifferent to her overtures of friendship.

"Good morning!" Kathy greeted the young girl. "Ready?"

Margot slouched into the room, giving Kathy a chilly look. "No—but does that really make any difference to you?" Her words and eyes were baiting. Kathy pretended not to notice.

"I have a job to do," she said. "How you feel *does* make a difference to me, but I have my obligations—"

"Oh, yes! Obligations!" Margot echoed in a scornful voice. "Just like mother has all *her* obligations . . ."

Kathy was surprised by her strong reaction. Beneath the disdain in Margot's voice was a strong hint of loneliness, a tinge of pathos. Kathy was perplexed. Did it actually bother Margot that Mrs. Jarrett was frequently away? Did the girl secretly wish her mother were around more—even as she seemed intent on alienating her?

"Take a seat, Margot," Kathy nodded toward the sitting area.

Sighing, resigned, Margot dropped into a chair. Kathy took a seat across from her, hoping that the informal setting might help Margot forget the distance between them.

The morning passed slowly, agonizingly. Margot Jarrett's attitude of mute disinterest made Kathy's job almost impossible. The girl ignored her questions, responding only after Kathy fed her the answers and succeeded in getting Margot to parrot them back to her.

The rest of the sessions that week, and the week following went no better. Guy was encouraging. Oatie tried to buoy Kathy's spirits. Mrs. Jarrett was openly appreciative. Jared was uncommunicative, his attitude growing more indifferent each day. Alana treated Kathy with as much warmth as Jared did cold disregard, until Kathy doubted her first impression that Alana was behind much of Margot's defiant behavior. But by the end of the first month, Kathy still saw no sign of progress in her student.

She was grateful for Guy's presence at the Ranch. He had become one of her best friends, and she knew she could always count on him for a cool, objective viewpoint. Many of her free evenings were spent in his company—sightseeing in the local area, talking quietly in the living room, or visiting with some of Guy's friends. His cheerfulness and optimism were good for Kathy, and she counted his friendship a special blessing.

Since Guy understood Margot so well, Kathy listened when he supported Margot's claim that she had studied even when Kathy suspected she had not. Nevertheless, by the middle of June, Kathy felt that the wages Mrs. Jarrett was paying her were wasted—not because she hadn't done her best, but because Margot Jarrett simply seemed to resist learning.

"I feel so much better about leaving on this trip—just knowing you're here, dear," Mrs. Jarrett countered. Her soft amber eyes glowed fondly as she regarded Kathy. "If you could have known Margot these last years . . . well, even Jared is impressed with what you have accomplished."

Kathy's heart skipped a beat at the mention of his name. Only a moment before she had felt discouragement bordering on despair. Knowing that Jared approved of the job she was doing made her feel almost giddy. Though she had seen him seldom since that evening on the porch, Jared Jarrett was never far from her thoughts.

"You'll answer to Jared while I'm away," Mrs. Jarrett was saying. "If you have any problems, I'll expect you to check with him. In my absence, what he says, goes."

"I don't expect to face anything I can't handle," she smiled, her confidence soaring.

CHAPTER 5

ON MRS. JARRETT'S second day away from home, Kathy consented to end Margot's study session early so Alana could take the girl shopping and out to lunch.

"You're a doll," Alana said when she came to collect Margot for the outing. "Thanks so much for doing me this favor."

"Have fun," Kathy said. "We can finish up tomorrow."

She waved them off and went into the kitchen to eat her light lunch alone. Mrs. Otis was already preparing dinner, the large meal of the day at the Ranch. Kathy was leaving the kitchen when Oatie invited her to ride to town to do some shopping.

"Thanks for the offer, Oatie, but not this time," Kathy refused. "I have a book I want to finish."

"Maybe next time," Oatie said, smiling.

It was pleasant having the place to herself. Kathy read for a while, then fell asleep with the book in her lap. She was sleeping soundly when the whirring noise of the vacuum sweeper in an adjoining room awakened her. Oatie shut off the noisy machine when Kathy appeared in the hallway.

"Have a good nap?" Mrs. Otis asked.

"Wonderful," Kathy replied, stretching. "But I feel like a piker sleeping away the afternoon while you work so hard."

"If you can fall asleep that easily, then I would say you needed the rest."

"Let me help you, Oatie. What can I do?"

"Nothing, honey," Oatie protested. "You're here to teach Margot—not do housework."

"But I'd like to help. I'm tired of reading or loafing by the pool."

"If you want to do something, lovey, be a dear and go to Mrs. Jarrett's room and get the watering can for the house plants. I think I left the can there when I cleaned."

When Kathy went downstairs to the master bedroom, she heard Alana's car in the drive. She had never been in Mrs. Jarrett's room before, and she was in the elegant quarters no longer than it took to fetch the ornately curved brass pot with the long, tapered spout.

"Bring the plant fertilizer up with you, too, Kathy," Oatie called down the stairs. "It's on the drainboard in the kitchen."

"All right," Kathy replied. The front door closed as she came out of Mrs. Jarrett's room and headed for the kitchen.

"Thanks so much, dearie," Mrs. Otis said when she and Kathy had finished up the light cleaning, placed the vacuum sweeper in the upstairs cleaning closet, and tucked away the other cleaning supplies.

"I enjoyed it," Kathy said. "A task is easier when it's shared."

"'Many hands make light work,'" quipped Oatie, laughing.

"Then how about some help with supper?" Kathy volunteered as she trailed behind Oatie into the charming kitchen.

"Well, there *are* some potatoes to be peeled."

The two women worked side-by-side in comfortable silence. It had been a long time since Kathy had felt free to work in a kitchen, and she had always liked to cook. No one would have dared enter the kitchen at Miss Atwood's without a special invitation from the temperamental cook.

"Jared's home," Oatie said, setting aside the vegetables she was cleaning. "I should find out if he's going to dine in tonight." Oatie called to Jared as he stepped in the front door.

"I don't think so, Oatie," he replied. "I have some important errands to take care of in town. I can get something at the Club. If I change my mind—I'll raid the refrigerator when I get home."

"See that you do!" Oatie said. She returned to the sink. "You've been looking peaked, Jared. I don't think you've been taking care of yourself."

"Oatie!" Jared sounded exasperated. "You and mother are a matched pair! Don't start on *that*. I'm fine! *Just fine.*"

Oatie winked at Kathy. "For being 'just fine,' Jared Matthew Jarrett, you're terribly testy of late!"

"And you, Oatie, my pet, are getting awfully sassy and insubordinate!" His chuckle removed the sting from his words. "But, I suppose, we wouldn't have you any other way."

"Ahh . . . flatterer!" Oatie groaned as Jared continued down the hall, laughing with good humor. His tone and attitude changed with the next breath.

"Oatie!" his voice grated. "Oatie—come here this minute! *Now!*"

Oatie dropped the vegetable brush, and wiped her hands on a dishtowel. With a puzzled glance in Kathy's direction, she hurried down the hall. Kathy followed her, and arrived in time to find Jared grilling the visibly upset housekeeper.

"You're sure you didn't move it, Oatie?" Jared asked harshly. "You're positive you didn't set it someplace for safekeeping?"

Oatie's eyes were wide with concern. Her face was pale; her lower lip trembled.

"Positive," she said. "Positive. I may be getting older, Jared Jarrett, but I haven't lost all my marbles. I can remember what I've done from one day to the next. I cleaned your mother's room the day she left, and today I stepped in only long enough to—''

"All right, all right!" Jared said shortly.

Jared knelt to look under the bed, then under the heavy dresser, and beneath the night table. With each movement, the frown on his face etched deeper.

"Is something lost?" Kathy asked.

"Mother's ring is missing," Jared answered sharply. "The Jarett ring." He dusted the knees of his slacks, stood up, and helped the pudgy housekeeper to her feet.

"I haven't seen it since the first night . . ." Kathy paused, embarrassed, recalling that painful scene.

"Well," Margot's word whistled in the air. "*I* most certainly haven't seen it." Kathy turned as the girl appeared behind her. She was chilled by the icy light in Margot's eyes.

"Where was it last seen?" Kathy asked, concerned.

"On mother's dresser," Jared said. "She laid it there the day she left. I had planned to take it to town to have the jeweler do some work on it." Jared gave Oatie another questioning look. "Pet, you're *sure* you didn't absentedly drop it into a drawer? A jewel box?" Oatie was almost in tears.

Her lip quivered. "Jared, I already told you—"

"All right, Oatie." Jared patted her plump arm. His frown grew stern. "It's just that valuable rings don't disappear by themselves. Do you think you might have knocked the ring from the dresser while you were cleaning?"

"Anything's possible, I suppose," Oatie said. "Let me get a flashlight and we'll look."

When she returned, Jared and Oatie scoured the room, probing into corners, beaming the ray of light beneath all the furniture.

"It's not here, Jared," Oatie said. "If it were—we'd have found it. It's . . ."

"*Gone,*" Jared supplied the word. From the dour expression on his face, and the tone of his voice, he might as well have said *stolen!* He turned on Kathy. "How about *you?* Have you been in this room?"

"I . . . was . . . only . . . but . . . not—" Kathy stammered, her face growing hot with embarrassment as her body chilled at the suggestions in his eyes. Jared's gaze was fierce, demanding, impatient.

"Yes or no?" he demanded. "Were you—or were you not—in mother's room?"

Before Kathy could find her voice, Margot spoke up, gloating.

"Yes, Jared—Miss Newby *was* in mother's room," Margot said. "I saw her coming out when I came home from shopping, but she didn't see me. I didn't bother to ask what she thought she was doing there . . ."

Oatie turned on Margot, her hands on her ample hips. "Wait a minute, Missie. I sent her to your mother's room to fetch the watering can for me. She was only in there for a moment."

"A moment is all it takes, Jared," Margot insinuated.

"Now don't go jumping to conclusions," Oatie warned. "That ring *must* be here somewhere." She flicked on the flashlight only to have Jared order her to shut it off.

"It's not in this room. You won't find it, Oatie, because it's not here; if it were, we'd have found it by now," he said.

Mrs. Otis, her face bewildered, her color ashen, returned to the kitchen. Kathy felt paralyzed.

"I—I hope the ring will turn up," she offered in a weak voice. Jared gave her a sharp glance. Margot spoke, her voice thick with sarcasm.

"I'm quite sure that's *exactly* what you're hoping, Miss Newby." Her eyes were mocking. "Maybe if you pray real hard, you'll get a miracle and—presto!—the Jarrett ring will appear on the dresser right before our very eyes."

"Margot!" Kathy was stricken by the raw hatred in the girl's voice, and the cruel knowledge that Margot was relishing her discomfort.

"Quit making sick jokes, Margot," Jared ordered in a flat voice. "The fact remains, rings don't magically reappear any more than they vanish on their own."

"No . . . they don't disappear on their own, do they, Jared?" Margot flung his thoughts back at him. She stuck her hands in her jeans pockets, rocked back on her heels, and stared at Kathy. "The Jarrett ring will probably turn up where we would *least* expect it."

Jared closed the door to Mrs. Jarrett's room. He was deeply disturbed. "I can't imagine . . ."

"Then you, Jared Jarrett, have a perfectly rotten imagination," Margot taunted. With that, his insolent little sister gave Kathy a calculated stare and stalked away.

Kathy felt Jared's eyes on her, but she couldn't see him for the brimming tears in her own eyes.

"We'll talk again in the morning, Miss Newby," Jared said in a low, cold voice, "when we've all had time to think. Perhaps by then the Jarrett ring will have . . . turned up . . . someplace."

He strode away and out the front door, leaving Kathy standing in the hallway. Behind Jared's careful words, she read the meaning. He was inviting her to return the ring to Mrs. Jarrett's room, or to put it someplace where it could be "found." Jared was kindly allowing her the opportunity to save face, for some reason, although it was clear he was convinced she had stolen the Jarrett ring. His words echoed with the unspoken warning that if she hadn't returned the ring by morning, or arranged for it to be found, he'd be forced to deal with her in the matter.

Sick at heart, her stomach tied in knots, Kathy slipped off to her room. When Oatie called her for dinner, she was too upset to consider food. Kathy knew that she should make an appearance, even if all she succeeded in doing was pushing the food around on her plate. But she couldn't bear the thought that even Oatie might be wondering if she'd misjudged Kathy, and that the new tutor was the thief she appeared to be.

The circumstantial evidence was heavily weighted against her. Forced to admit she had been in Mrs. Jarrett's room, she seemed the most likely candidate. And with Mrs. Jarrett away, and Jared in complete control, Kathy knew that if the ring didn't "magically and miraculously" reappear by morning, she would be fired without a moment's hesitation. By the time Mrs. Jarrett returned, another tutor would have "bitten the dust."

Kathy decided that, before she would give Jared Jarrett the pleasure of firing her, she would resign. Let him think whatever he pleased, she and the Lord knew the truth.

Guy would understand her resignation. He knew her well—better even than did Mrs. Otis. Guy would know she was innocent of any wrongdoing. *So,* Kathy thought, *would Margot Jarrett!*

Once Kathy had made up her mind, she emptied her dresser methodically, took her small wardrobe from the closet, and packed her suitcase. Taking her cosmetics case into the adjoining bath to collect her personal items, she folded a pair of hose she'd laundered by hand and hung on the shower rack to dry. As she tucked them into the elasticized pocket of the small case, she touched something cold and hard. She searched the stretchy pocket, found the object, and pulled it out, staring—dazed.

It was the Jarrett ring!

The large stone twinkled and the smaller diamonds flashed with fiery light. Kathy's heart soared—it was like a miracle! Then her spirits plummeted as she understood the implications. The Jarrett ring had been found . . . in a place "we would least expect it to be!"

Kathy stared blindly at the ring. Margot's ploy was as transparent as the sparkling stone. If Kathy resigned, Jared would have undoubtedly searched Kathy's things at Margot's suggestion. The Jarrett ring would have been found in her possession. If the ring had gone undetected by Kathy, and Jared hadn't bothered to conduct a search, it would have never shown up and everyone would have assumed Kathy *had* stolen the ring. If, at a later date, Kathy discovered the ring and returned it, she would appear to have experienced a change of heart. Even now, bringing it forth would place her under suspicion. Though nothing more would be said, she knew that she would never again be trusted. It was a no-win situation.

Kathy examined the beautiful ring, and wished desperately that she could return it to Jared and conclude the unpleasant business.

She stayed up late, pacing the floor in her room while she waited for Jared's return. Minutes dragged into hours. By two o'clock in the morning, Kathy decided Jared probably wasn't coming home. Reluctantly she went to bed, to spend what was left of the night in sleepless turmoil.

Early the next morning, Kathy slipped downstairs, hoping Mrs. Otis wouldn't hear her and admonish her to eat before she could take up the matter of the Jarrett ring with Jared.

Kathy hurried past the kitchen and down the hall to his office. The door was closed, but the noise coming from within signaled his presence. She knocked boldly.

"Come in," Jared said.

Her heart pounding, Kathy entered Jared's office. Words of explanation whirled in her mind. But they stubbornly refused to form a coherent sentence.

Jared was on the telephone and quickly excused himself when he saw Kathy. Carefully he replaced the receiver in the cradle, then leaned back in his desk chair and stared at her, gesturing impatiently for her to close the door and be seated.

"May I talk to you for a few minutes?" Kathy asked, dismayed at the timidity of her voice.

Jared was brusque. "Saves my having to send for you."

Kathy winced at the meaning of his words. She took a deep breath and prayed that she would find the right words.

"About the Jarrett ring . . . I found it last night."

Jared showed no surprise. "May I have it?" he asked flatly, holding out his hand.

"Yes—of course."

Kathy produced the ring from the pocket of her dress. Jared took it, casually examined it, then turned his smoldering gaze on Kathy.

"There's been a mistake, Mr. Jarrett," Kathy plunged ahead before he could speak. "A trick. You might not choose to believe this, but I'm quite positive that Margot took your mother's ring and hid it with my belongings. No one was more surprised than I when I found it in my suitcase as I was packing to leave."

"You're leaving?"

Kathy nodded, then shook her head in confusion. "I *was* going to resign, and I still *will*, if you want me to. You have the ring back and that's what matters. I can leave in peace knowing in my heart that I'm innocent." Kathy's voice grew bolder, her words more confident. "It matters little to me what you—or anyone else—may think about me so long as *I* know the truth." Kathy hesitated. "My bags are packed—I can leave now. But the thought came to me during the night that if I do leave, or if you send me away—then Margot can claim another victory. She'll have succeeded in getting rid of me . . . ."

Realization dawned over Jared's features, his doubtful expression giving way to grim knowledge. He regarded the Jarrett ring, then casually slipped it in his pocket, sighing.

"I believe you," he said quietly. Then he smiled ruefully. "To be the innocent victim of a cruel prank, Kathy, you did a terrific job of *acting* very guilty!"

Kathy felt flustered even though Jared's eyes were now teasing instead of accusing. "It's not easy when everyone else views you as a thief."

"I suppose not," Jared agreed. "But not everyone holds that view. Oatie told me this morning she was positive you were innocent. She told me that you were too committed to Christian principles to steal." Jared's voice grew acid. "Not that *that* line of reasoning swayed me in the least. In my lifetime I've known too many 'good' Christians who've done some rather disgusting things."

"I'm glad, at least, to know Oatie believed me," Kathy said.

"She does. I do, too, *now,*" Jared said, "if belated belief is any consolation."

Kathy forced a weak smile. "It's never too late to believe. It helps to know that your faith in me has been restored."

Jared arose and crossed the room to where Kathy stood by the window. "I really don't know what to do about Margot," he sighed pensively. "She must have been desperate to be rid of you to stoop to something so . . . *low*. She drove away all the others much more quickly—and with less effort."

"I'm not all the others," Kathy said pointedly.

"No," Jared breathed softly. He turned to Kathy and looked at her as if he were truly seeing her for the first time. His eyes swept her like an intimate caress. His voice was husky when he spoke. "No, Kathy Newby, you're not like all the others, You're very special . . ."

Jared stared down at Kathy, a rush of strong emotions overwhelming him. She looked up at him, her slight trembling betraying her feelings. She turned away from him, shaken.

"It's time for me to go to my office," she said. "I—I have lessons to plan. Margot won't get out of studying as easily as she thinks," Kathy added, attempting to fill the tense silence that enveloped them.

As she turned to leave, Jared, unable to restrain himself, stopped her. She did not resist his touch.

Suddenly, Jared Jarrett, who had mastered many women as easily as he tamed the wild horses on the Ranch, was at a loss for words. None of the glib phrases that at other times came so readily to his lips seemed appropriate.

Before Kathy knew what was happening, she was in Jared's arms, returning his kisses with an ardor that matched his own. She thrilled to the sensation of being engulfed by his towering presence—his rugged manly body, as angular and hard as hers was soft and yielding. He murmured tender words. Then his kisses grew more demanding, almost brutal with passion, before his lips left Kathy's to trail across her cheek to the warm hollow of her slim neck. Her breath quickened. She felt her limbs grow weak, and she swayed

62

against Jared as the world spun dizzily around her.

"Jared . . . *no!*" Kathy whispered, pleading, struggling to free herself from his embrace, even as she wanted to lose herself in the circle of his arms.

In answer, Jared returned her to his savage embrace. Kathy resisted at first, knowing she was no match for his strength. Helplessly, shamelessly, she surrendered to Jared's tender kisses, awakening desires that long had lain dormant. His lips were the first to break away, and when he looked at Kathy, his eyes were agonized, his breathing ragged. He released her, as if he couldn't trust himself to touch her again.

"Kathy . . . my darling . . ." His eyes grew moist with longing. Slowly she recovered her composure. Her fingers touched her lips, still burning from Jared's kisses. She looked away, cheeks flushed with emotion and embarrassment.

"We mustn't . . ." she whispered.

"Perhaps not," Jared murmured. "But don't expect me to apologize, because I won't. I don't regret kissing you any more than you regretted my doing so!"

Kathy was deeply shaken. She wanted to deny it, to tell him that she did regret it. But she couldn't deny the truth that, at that moment, more than anything else, she wanted to be back in his arms again.

"I'd better find Margot," Kathy said in a faint voice, and fled before Jared could stop her.

He watched her small form retreating from his office with a curious mixture of reluctance and relief. As he sank into his chair, he weighed his emotions, deciding it was in his best interests that this irresistible girl had left before he said or did something they would both later regret. Before he made promises to himself—or to her—that he knew he could never keep.

Jared slammed his fist on the desk. The paperweight jumped with the impact. He muttered an oath, then leaned back, closing his eyes wearily.

If only Kathy were different! If only *he* were different! Much as he wanted her, Jared knew Kathy Newby could no more change to suit his needs than he could change to fulfill her dreams.

The telephone at his elbow shrilled, jarring him from his inner turmoil. His voice was gruff when he answered, registering his impatience at the interruption. His voice softened when he recognized Alana's voice. The troubled frown was replaced by a light smile.

"I was just thinking about you, pet," Jared said.

Alana laughed, pleased. "Make sure you keep thinking of me, darling," she commanded.

"It's a promise."

That was one vow he could keep. Alana Fontaine was the perfect antidote to his addiction to Kathy Newby. As he listened to Alana's plans for an expensive evening on the town, the memory of Kathy's sweet, yielding lips, and the soft contours of her slim body began to fade, then disappeared altogether when Alana wickedly hinted at what lay in store following dinner and dancing.

Before he turned back to his work, Jared decided it hadn't hurt to entertain a few thoughts about Kathy, or to exchange a kiss or two, so long as he understood that idle fancy was all it would ever be. The girl was enticing and attractive, but Alana Fontaine was the perfect woman for him.

He and Alana understood each other. She was as passionate as he and had no rigid code of ethics that got in the way of a good time. She made no demands that Jared couldn't easily fulfill, and she was intelligent enough never to insist he love her or even pretend he did. Alana gave him the things a man wanted, when he wanted them; in return, he gave her all the luxuries that the Jarrett money could buy.

Jared's hand touched the ring in his pocket. In time, he would give Alana the Jarrett ring and his name as well, he decided. Granted, Alana was headstrong and deceitful and she possessed a number of deliciously devilish flaws. But her weaknesses were no worse than his own. They made a good pair—a very good pair. They were both pragmatic people with the good sense never to expect more from a relationship than the other could willingly give . . .

CHAPTER 6

MARGOT OFFERED NO ARGUMENT when Kathy located her near a corral and informed her that classes would begin in five minutes. When Kathy turned on her heel, she could feel Margot's eyes boring into her back, but the defiant girl arrived on time.

Although Margot was far from cooperative, neither was she quite as antagonistic, which led Kathy to wonder if Margot was feeling some remorse for what she had done.

"Read the next chapter for tomorrow, Margot," she instructed. "We'll discuss it then."

Sighing with boredom, but without her usual smart remark, Margot left the room. Kathy remained in her office to put away materials before going outside for a breath of fresh air. When Kathy reached the front door, it opened upon her and she was forced to jump aside.

"Sorry, Kathy!" Guy said with a grin. "I didn't mean to bowl you over. At least not *that* way!"

Kathy's delight in seeing Guy for the first time in several days did not go unnoticed by the tall foreman.

"Looking for Jared?" she asked.

Guy shook his head. "For *you*." He checked his watch.

"I've only got a few minutes before we take the jeep out to the pasture to fix some fences the mustangs tore down, but I wanted to stop by the house and see if you're free tonight. The church youth group is having a hayride. Bootsy Holloway called the bunkhouse this morning and asked if I could help chaperone the party tonight. It seems someone got sick at the last minute. I'd like you to go with me."

Kathy accepted without hesitation. "I'd love to. It sounds like fun."

In the weeks Kathy had been at the Ranch, she had met some of the young people and adults near her own age after Sunday services and on the occasional evenings when she had gone with Guy to visit his friends. She felt as comfortable with these people as she did with Guy.

"Terrific! I'll pick you up about seven. Wear something comfortable."

"Oh-oh!" Kathy groaned.

At the sound of the dismay in her voice, Guy turned back to her, concerned.

"What's wrong?"

"I know this sounds 'just like a woman,' but I haven't a thing to wear! I lost my jeans and shirts in the fire and the clothes I've been buying are not appropriate for a hayride. So, Guy, I'm sorry, but I'll have to pass . . ."

"No problem," he said "Excuse me a minute."

Before she could question him, Guy left her standing in the foyer, exited through the swinging doors into the kitchen, and spoke to Oatie. She heard the back door slam behind him. A minute later Guy surprised Kathy by reappearing at the front door.

"You're all set," he said. "I asked a favor of an old . . . pal of mine. Margot will bring some duds to your room. If they fit—wear 'em."

"Margot?"

"Sure! Why not?" Guy asked lightly. "She and I were good friends at one time. I figured if I asked her, she'd help me out in a pinch." Guy touched Kathy's cheek, his voice dropped. "I know Margot's been treating you pretty shabbily, but try to remember that beneath that tough-lady act, there's a confused young kid who wants to be good—and needs to be liked."

"Sometimes it's easier to forget that than it is to remember it," Kathy said, with a wry smile.

"I've asked Margot several times to go to the hayride. I just asked her again. She said she'd think it over—which *is* progress from a flat no. I don't suppose she'll break down and go," Guy sighed. "But you might mention it to her when she brings you the jeans."

"I will," she promised.

Guy grinned. "Good. I'll see you tonight."

Less than an hour later Kathy was in her room writing a letter to Trish Nobel when there was a soft knock on her door.

"Come in," she invited.

It was the first time Margot had ventured into Kathy's room when she was there, although Kathy knew Margot had probably visited her room several times when she was not.

Margot's face was unemotional, her voice, indifferent. "Guy said you needed some clothes." Margot dumped several pairs of jeans on Kathy's bed. "Maybe these'll fit."

"How nice of you, Margot! I'll try them on right away." When the girl turned to leave, Kathy asked her to stay so that "If they don't fit, you can take them back now." Margot sat down on the edge of the bed as Kathy disappeared into the adjoining bath.

"The burgundy pair fits perfectly," Kathy called. "Thanks so much. I really appreciate your loaning me something to wear tonight."

Kathy entered the room, modeling the jeans for Margot's inspection. The younger girl swept a lock of hair away from her face and over her shoulder. "Guy asked me to . . ."

It was clear that Margot wanted Kathy to know that her gesture had been for Guy's sake, not for her benefit. Kathy shrugged and smiled warmly.

"I appreciate it just the same. There's something else Guy would really like for you to do."

67

"What?" Margot's brows knit together with suspicion.

"Go along with us tonight. I'd like that, too. Hayrides are so much fun!"

Margot thought for only a moment, then she tilted her chin stubbornly. "I don't want to go—and I don't have to go."

"That's up to you. Guy says the kids . . ."

"The 'kids' are immature, unsophisticated babies!" Margot snapped.

"I should think you might get lonely here," Kathy chose her words carefully. "With no one your own age on the Ranch, and no friends coming to see you . . ."

Margot's steely gaze wavered. Then through clenched teeth, she muttered, "I have all the friends I need," she said coldly. "Alana is my best friend. She treats me like a grown-up, not like some dumb little kid. Alana's more fun than those babies in the church youth group. I don't need them." Margot's voice cracked with anger. She tossed her head, her hair flying. "Any more than they need *me*."

"That's your decision," Kathy said. "But you *are* invited."

Margot turned to go, the conversation ended. Then she asked unexpectedly, "Have you got shoes? You can't wear those on a hayride."

"Right you are," Kathy admitted, wondering if there was time to drive into town to buy a pair of canvas shoes.

"Don't get uptight," Margot said. "I have some old riding boots I've outgrown. I think they might fit you. They're in my room."

Accepting the statement as an invitation, Kathy followed Margot to her room. It was a typical teen-aged girl's room, but missing was the happy clutter of a carefree student kept busy by school activities. There were no game pennants. No classmates' pictures tucked into the vanity mirror. No stuffed mascot on the dresser. There was something lonely about the lovely room with its designer decor, expensive stereo equipment, miniature portable television, and luxurious appointments.

Margot crossed the room to the closet and plucked a pair of brown suede boots from the dark recesses.

"Here."

She held out the boots to Kathy and swept her long hair away from her face with a quick, graceful gesture. Kathy was struck again by Margot's pretty face, soft and vulnerable, and momentarily minus the usual hard defiant lines.

"Thanks," Kathy said, hopeful that this might be the opportunity she had been waiting for. Perhaps Margot was ready to accept her friendship—to talk—about anything. But Kathy's hopes were dashed when Margot's next brusque words made it clear she wanted to be left alone. Deep in her heart, Kathy wondered if Margot Jarrett didn't reject other people—before they had a chance to reject her.

Kathy was ready and waiting when Guy picked her up for the drive to the country church where Mrs. Jarrett and many of her neighbors attended services. Guy parked his car in the lot and, together, they greeted the group gathered around picnic tables.

"Isn't it a perfect night for a hayride?" Bootsy Holloway asked.

"Lovely," Kathy agreed. "Can I help?"

"You can lend a hand laying out the supplies." Bootsy gave the men a glance. "They guys will get the bonfire going now so the embers will be just right when we get back."

Kathy helped Bootsy unpack the hampers and thought again what a pity it was Margot hadn't come along. The young girl couldn't have helped enjoying the company of the teen-agers who were laughing and talking in clusters.

Soon three tractors pulling hayracks laden with straw appeared. The young people and adult chaperones clambered onto the wagons that jolted ahead, shaking wisps of straw to the ground.

Guy put his hands on Kathy's slim waist and lifted her onto the hayrack where Bootsy and her husband Wayne were already seated.

"It's too bad Margot wouldn't come with us," Guy said.

Several of the neighborhood children attacked Guy, stuffing straw down the back of his shirt until he wrestled them off and leaned back against the wagon brace, laughing as he caught his breath. He slipped his arm around Kathy.

"By the way—what's wrong with Jared?"

Kathy faced Guy in the soft twilight. "What do you mean?"

Guy hesitated only a moment. "He hasn't been fit to live with the past few days. The men are starting to grumble to me—but there's not much I can do. Jared's been as curt with me as he has with them. In fact, more so. A few of the ranch hands are already making remarks about moving on."

"That's too bad."

"It really is, because the hands we have now are top-notch workers. They've got it good at the Black Diamond, so they don't want to leave—but they *will* if Jared doesn't slack off."

"Have you told him that?"

Guy laughed shortly. "In his present state—I haven't dared. Jared and I go back a lot of years and we've always gotten along very well until lately. I swear I can't figure it out. Something's bothering him, but I have no idea what it is." He searched Kathy's face. "Has something happened at the Big House?"

"Well . . . maybe," she sighed. Quietly, so the others wouldn't overhear, Kathy told Guy about Margot's attempt to make her look like a thief and Jared's reaction. She expected Guy to be outraged by Margot's treachery, and was surprised when he showed more interest in the plans to take the ring to the jeweler than in her painful predicament.

"So that's it!" He gave a low, meaningful whistle. "Now it makes sense. Knowing that the Jarrett ring is involved makes Jared's moodiness forgivable. Understandable. I'd probably be nervous in that situation, too." Guy's mood buoyed. "I was afraid Jared was upset with me personally."

Before Kathy could ask Guy what was so important about the Jarrett ring, Bootsy and Wayne shifted in the straw and drew near. While the men discussed ranching, Kathy and Bootsy chatted.

"This is fun," Bootsy said. "I enjoy the hayrides as much now as I did when I was a teen-ager and Wayne and I were dating."

"You've always lived nearby?" Kathy asked.

"All my life. So has Wayne." Bootsy tossed her brown hair away from her face. "My dad has a small spread near the old Fontaine Ranch."

"I suppose you know Alana well?"

Bootsy laughed. "Perhaps *too* well." From the expression of exasperation on her face, Kathy sensed Bootsy didn't have much regard for the beautiful, coppery-haired woman. "Do you run into Alana often now that she and Jared are seeing so much of each other?"

"Occasionally," Kathy replied. "I scarcely know her, although she's been very pleasant to me when we do meet." Except for the horrid first evening, it was true. Alana had been a different person altogether.

"Alana and I used to be friends—after a fashion—when her folks still owned the Lone Star." Bootsy continued. "But after her dad lost all his money and the ranch as well, Alana went East. We move in different worlds, I guess, and I rarely see her anymore."

"The Fontaines lost the Lone Star?" Kathy asked, incredulous.

From the few comments she had heard, Kathy assumed that Alana was as wealthy as Jared Jarrett.

"Alana and I were in high school together." Bootsy explained, "It caused a real stir in the area when Mr. Fontaine went to Las Vegas a rich man and returned a poor one. Some people said he had a compulsion to gamble." Bootsy shrugged. "Maybe he did. The bottom line is that he lost the Lone Star and all his holdings."

"How sad."

"It was sad. Mr. Fontaine was one of the wealthiest men in the area and almost overnight he had nothing. Poor Alana. She could hardly bear to face everyone at school, living in a run-down rented place on the edge of town, after the fancy ranch house. And she was ashamed, you could tell, when her dad took a job at the grain elevator in town."

"It must've been a blow to them."

"More than Mr. Fontaine could stand. He committed suicide a few months later, and left Alana and her mother almost penniless except for what Mrs. Fontaine realized from the settlement of her parents' estate. She opened a boutique, bought a house on the edge of town where Alana could keep a horse, and packed Alana off to a fancy school back East."

Kathy was puzzled. "It seems odd she'd spend the money to send Alana away to school if she couldn't afford it."

Bootsy laughed. "She felt they couldn't afford *not* to send her! You've heard the old saying, 'To have money, one must spend money'? Well, Alana's always been a pretty girl, and the very rich girls at a ritzy boarding school might just happen to have some very rich brothers! It was a scheme to marry Alana off in the style to which she had once been accustomed."

Kathy was appalled. "You can't be serious!"

"But I am," Bootsy said. "Alana wasn't as successful in snagging a rich husband as hoped. When she returned from Boston, she found Jared Jarrett home from a stint in the Navy. Everyone knows that once she becomes Mrs. Jared Jarrett, she'll have all the money she could ever want. She'll set up an apartment in the East and divide her time between Jared and the Black Diamond Ranch, and her ritzy friends back East."

Kathy found it hard to believe that anyone could be so calculating—so mercenary—but Guy echoed Bootsy's opinions on the drive home.

"Bootsy is right. Alana will marry Jared and get the financial security she wants. In return, she will serve as his wife and hostess when he needs her, and jet East when he doesn't."

"But doesn't Alana love Jared?" Kathy asked.

Guy chuckled, amused at the idea. "Of course not! No more than Jared loves her. Alana loves only one thing—money. Jared's at an age, thirty-three, when he has no doubt begun to entertain thoughts of marriage." Guy gave his lovely companion a studied glance. "I think about it more and more often myself. Jared, apparently, has decided to do more than *think* about getting married."

So Guy thought about marriage? And who would be the lucky girl? Kathy wondered. Carolyn Meyers seemed the most logical choice. Bootsy had confided that Guy had seemed quite serious about the attractive secretary when she came to visit the Holloways. Guy spent every spare minute at the Holloway ranch with Carolyn when she was in the area. If Guy loved Carolyn, Kathy knew immediately she was a very lucky woman.

"We're home," Guy said, pulling the car to a stop.

Kathy yawned as Guy helped her from the car. "This was so much fun, Guy, I can't remember the last time I had such an enjoyable evening."

"I enjoyed it, too." Guy's voice became a husky whisper. "Mostly because you were with me, Kathy."

"How sweet of you to say that!"

"It's not flattery—or a line I use on all the women I meet," Guy said seriously. "Tonight was different for me because I was with you. You're very special to me."

"You're special to me, too, Guy," Kathy admitted.

It *was* true. Guy Armitage was the kind of friend who offered an easy, comfortable relationship characteristic of people committed to Christ. Guy was important to her in that way and . . . Jared Jarrett, in quite another.

Jared!

His image was strong in her thoughts as Guy's lips touched hers. It was a sweet kiss—tender and cherishing. This almost reverent caress scarcely evoked the same heady response as Jared's kiss of earlier that morning. His lips had been possessive, demanding, and she had been swept into a delicious maelstrom of desire. For a desperate moment, Kathy wished that she could feel that same wild abandon

73

with Guy. He was a decent man, who shared her Christian beliefs and goals.

Even as he held her close, the recognition dawned that Guy's thoughts of marriage no longer included Carolyn Meyers, if, indeed, they ever had. Guy was in love with Kathy! And neither that knowledge nor the tenderness of his caresses could extinguish the burning brand of Jared's imprint on her lips, her mind, her heart . . .

Car lights arched over the patio, imprisoning Guy and Kathy in the bright beam. They parted quickly.

"Good night, Kathy," he whispered.

"Night, Guy. And thanks for a wonderful evening."

Kathy slipped into the house. She had barely closed the door behind her when she heard the staccato rhythm of Jared's steps on the walk. Guy spoke to him as they passed, and Jared responded curtly. Guy was right—he *was* cranky!

Kathy was in the living room when Jared entered the house—slamming the door behind him. She halted at the staircase and looked back to see Jared silhouetted in the foyer.

"Good evening, Jared," Kathy said, disturbed by the savage light in his eyes. He gave her a long, mocking look.

"Maybe for some people it was a good evening. Did you enjoy your romantic hayride?" His voice was sarcastic.

"What business is it of yours?" Kathy started to fling the words in his face, but instead, she swallowed the sharp retort.

"Yes, Jared, very much. Thanks to Guy, I had a lovely evening."

"I'm sure he saw to that—if the exhibition on the front step was any indication!"

Kathy's face colored hotly. "If you'll excuse me, I'm going to my room—now that you've assured yourself of my welfare, although it's hardly your concern since evenings *are* my own."

"Yes, they are. You can spend them wherever you like, with whomever you like . . . doing whatever you like."

Jared's words sent a surge of anger boiling near the surface. He had managed to make the innocent occasion seem like a tawdry affair. Something to be ashamed of. "Good night—*Mr. Jarrett*," she said abruptly.

Jared's mouth opened, then closed, as if he were about to say something else, then thought better of it. With a scowl in Kathy's direction, he turned abruptly and strode down the hall to his office, banging the door shut with a resounding crack. His chair creaked across the floor and his booted feet hit the familiar corner of his desk with a thud.

What a state Jared is in! Kathy thought. No wonder Guy and the hands were upset. Jared had made her feel as if she, too, were the basis for all his problems and irritations.

Kathy saw little of Jared the next day. Or the next. How awful it must be for Guy, who had to work closely with him day in and day out, she thought. It was no wonder Guy was hurt after all the years of intimate friendship—or that the other hands who owed no real allegiance to the Jarretts or the Black Diamond were murmuring about moving on to positions elsewhere.

In the following days, as Kathy observed Jared's fits of temper and melancholy, she experienced a stirring of sympathy for the troubled man. Like Margot, he was thrashing like a wild mustang, seemingly resisting a Force beyond himself—unwilling to surrender the reins. But Kathy had to admit that, except for her first evening at the Ranch, when Jared had been unquestionably rude, she had been impressed by the flair and finesse with which he transacted business and handled social situations. He easily made the transition from the ranch office, where he dealt with businessmen in three-piece suits, to the fields and corrals, where he would appear in rugged work clothes to labor side by side with his men, of whom he never asked more than he willingly gave himself.

The Jared of past weeks was very unlike this irascible tyrant, lashing out without provocation at old and trusted employees. He needed her prayers, not her wrath.

Lord, grant me the patience and understanding to cope

with Jared's moods, Kathy prayed. *Help me to control my own emotions, and strengthen me when I'm weak and hurting.*

Then, as always, she prayed for Margot, Mrs. Jarrett, Oatie, Guy—for all the people in her new world. Then she added one more urgent prayer—that the Lord would remove from her heart the passionate feelings she had for Jared Jarrett.

Such a love could never be. Jared was not a Christian. She could not imagine his submitting to any authority—human or divine. His proud nature demanded that he be master of all he surveyed—whether the lush, rolling acres of the Black Diamond or the lives of the people around him.

As much as Kathy was irresistibly drawn to Jared, there was no turning back, no denying the promise she had made long ago—that she would never be unequally yoked to an unbeliever—not even if his name was Jared Jarrett!

CHAPTER 7

JARED'S DOOR WAS CLOSED when Kathy arrived in her office to prepare for the study session with Margot. She had brought the freshly laundered jeans and the borrowed riding boots to return to her student.

"Thanks again, Margot," Kathy smiled, when the slight blonde entered the room. "I don't know what I would have done last night without your clothes."

Margot took her chair. "Keep them," she said shortly, not lifting her eyes. "You may need them . . . again."

Kathy's heart soared. The girl's words were a sign—however small—that she was beginning to accept her presence. The remark validated Kathy's belief that some positive changes were beginning to manifest themselves in Margot. Unfortunately, her older brother's attitude seemed to be taking a turn for the worse.

In the past week's time Jared had kept Guy so busy that Kathy had scarcely seen the tall foreman except when he accompanied the rest of them to church on Sunday morning. She found herself missing Guy's pleasant company in the evening, but she understood he needed his rest more than ever.

Kathy was thus surprised and delighted when one morning, after Guy had by-passed her office enroute to Jared's, only to find the Boss gone, he stopped in to see her on his way back.

"How are things going with Margot?" he asked.

Kathy's smile was bright. "*Very* well! She's not exactly bucking for the title of 'Teacher's Pet' yet, but she's not the handful she was. We get along—or at least she's declared a truce of some sort. How are things with you—and Jared?"

Guy shrugged and forced a smile. "So-so, Kath," he sighed. A shadow crept across his features. "Actually, not good. Not good at all," he admitted. "I've been putting off seeing Jared about the situation in hopes he'd get over what's bothering him, but he hasn't. I made up my mind this morning to bring things to a showdown."

Kathy knew that Guy was justified in his stand. Jared had been so testy in his dealings with Guy that any other hand would have tendered a resignation long before. But she changed the subject, hoping to alleviate Guy's bitterness with some light-hearted small talk. She wanted to make him laugh again—see him smile.

Guy was chuckling over something Kathy had said as he leaned against the corner of her desk and watched her fondly. She smiled up at him, her eyes sparkling. Neither of them heard the front door open and close. Neither of them heard footsteps in the hall—or knew anyone was present until Jared Jarrett made his appearance known! Simultaneously they stared at the open doorway.

Jared, his face stony, his dark eyes a stern reprimand, spoke harshly. "Your noon hour hasn't begun yet, Guy." His words were biting. Guy stiffened with fresh anger. Kathy knew that he was thinking of the many times when, on his own time and expecting no compensation, he had stayed up all night with a sick cow or an injured horse, or had made extra trips to the pastures in raging blizzards to make sure the livestock was safe.

Kathy sensed that the moment of reckoning was fast approaching. She knew that if Guy lost control for an instant and exploded with fury, Jared would fire him on the spot—and relish the task! She hoped Guy would have the chance to resign with dignity. She placed a restraining hand on his arm. Guy glanced into her eyes, and saw the support there. He sagged slightly as the hot anger ebbed away. Jared gave Kathy a withering look.

"I might remind you *both*," Jared said, "that neither of you were employed by the Black Diamond to socialize. You were hired to perform specific tasks, and I suggest you both attend to your own business. Entertain each other on your own time—*not mine!*"

Guy lunged for Jared, his eyes sparking. Jared assessed Guy with a mocking gaze. His eyes were a taunting dare. Kathy kept her grip on Guy's arm. "Kath . . . can I see you tonight?" Guy said under his breath. She squeezed his arm encouragingly.

"Sure," she whispered.

Guy jammed the Stetson on his head and with an icy glance at Jared, swung past the tall rancher, his back ramrod-stiff.

Kathy felt Jared's gaze burn over her, but thankfully he proceeded down the hall into his office, where he remained for only a moment before he stormed out again. Mrs. Otis was on her way to summon Kathy for lunch, and when she asked Jared if he wanted something to eat, he almost snapped her head off.

Oatie stepped into Kathy's office and halted in the open doorway to stare after Jared. "He's in a fine state, isn't he?" Oatie asked.

"He certainly is. Oatie—you've been with the Jarretts a lot of years and you probably know Jared as well as anyone. What on earth is wrong with him? He has hurt Guy so badly that he's going to lose him."

Mrs. Otis glanced toward Mrs. Jarrett's office that had remained closed throughout the fracas, then closed Kathy's door behind her.

"I *do* know what's bothering Jared," Oatie said in a confidential whisper. She plucked a few dead leaves from a plant in the windowsill as she allowed the suspense to build.

"What, pray tell?" Kathy prodded.

Oatie grinned. "Jared Jarrett is positively pea-green with jealousy. That's what's wrong with him!"

"Jealous? Of whom?"

"Of *Guy*."

"Guy? Whatever for?"

Oatie was smug. "Because Guy's sweet on you, Kathy, and you're paying attention to him. It's driving Jared wild." The sound of Oatie's laugh was like a trilling bird. "Mrs. Jarrett's plan is working—that's for sure."

Kathy was suspicious. "Plan . . . Oatie? I don't understand. What plan are you talking about?"

"Of course you don't understand," Oatie waved a plump hand. "Maybe not a *real plan*—because Mrs. J. isn't the conniving type—but I'll bet you weren't hired just to tutor Margot Jarrett," Oatie paused. "I'm a mother, too—and I'd have done the same thing to save one of my boys from marrying the wrong woman—particularly one as money-hungry and calculating as Alana Fontaine. I think Mrs. Jarrett brought you here—a pretty, smart, fine Christian—so that Jared could see what *real* wife material looks like!"

Kathy's face stained deep crimson. "Oatie, you've been watching too many daytime dramas on television."

"No, I haven't!" Oatie sniffed. "I know Mrs. Jarrett brought you here to help Margot, but it's a neat trick if she can help her son as well."

Kathy thought back to the day in Mr. Stockton's office at the Archway Employment Agency. It *had* been puzzling that physical attractiveness had been a rigid requirement. Could there be something to Oatie's ideas? But Jared had seemed intent on avoiding her since the morning he'd kissed her in his office. His aloofness was hardly the attitude of an admirer!

"I think you were out in the sun too long this morning, Oatie," Kathy smiled.

"Bosh!" The cook snorted with indignation. "I've been around long enough to know what's going on. Guy Armitage thinks you're the cat's meow. So does Jared, though I suspect Jared would have a fit if he knew I had him figured out. Jared's involved wth Alana, so he can't make a play for you. It's infuriating him that Guy's beating his time.''

"I like Guy very much, Oatie, but only as a friend.''

"I know *that*,'' Oatie said smugly. Her eyes narrowed in thought. "But I don't think Guy does. And it's a sure thing Jared doesn't know that Guy's 'only a friend.' If he did, he wouldn't be as testy as a teased rattlesnake. I'll bet Jared's played with the idea of firing Guy just to remove the competition.''

"He wouldn't—''

"No,'' Oatie said, positive. "He would never get away with it. Victoria Jarrett gives Jared free hand in running the Ranch, but she does have the final say around here. And she loves Guy Armitage like a son.'

"This is all an interesting theory, Oatie, but it doesn't really make sense.''

"Yes, it does!'' Oatie protested. "Who is a man like Jared to date around here? He's much too old for the high-school girls. And most of the women his own age have been married for years. There simply aren't many eligible women in these parts.''

"There are suitable women elsewhere, I'm sure.''

Oatie laughed it off. "Jared rarely goes 'elsewhere.' He loves this ranch. Sure, he goes to cattlemen's meetings, livestock sales, a few rodeos, but you don't expect him to find a wife in a world of men! The truth is, Kathy, Jared Jarrett has had to . . . *make do* . . . with what's been available—Alana Fontaine. What is that old saying?'' Oatie frowned in thought. "Something about 'If Mohammed won't go to the mountain—then you take the mountain to Mohammed'? Mrs. J. brought you here—and none too soon, if you ask me!''

"You sound like a frustrated matchmaker. You seem to forget that Jared hasn't exactly showered me with attention.''

"Horsefeathers! Just like a man!'' Oatie said. "Doesn't

even know his own mind. Maybe Jared thinks he has no interest in you—but *I* know better. He's fighting the feelings he has for you—just like you're battling the feelings *you* have for *him*."

Kathy was caught off guard. "I have no feelings for him other than those I'd have for any other . . . *employer*."

In answer Oatie grinned impishly. "Maybe you've convinced yourself of that, Kathy dear, but you'll never convince *me*." Mrs. Otis looked wistful "It would do my old heart good—Mrs. J's, too—if you'd admit how you feel and give Alana a run for her money!"

"I'd never do that!" Kathy cried. "I've never chased a man in my life—and I don't intend to start now!"

Oatie's eyes twinkled. "I know you wouldn't. That's part of what makes you so appealing to me, to Victoria, to Guy, but most of all to Jared. You're the *real thing*, Kathy. A lady! The kind of woman a man wants for his wife. I only hope that Jared Jarrett realizes it before he gets himself engaged to that Fontaine hussy!"

Oatie left the office, her laughter floating in the air. Kathy sank into her desk chair, too shaky from Oatie's revelations to trust her legs to support her. She was more than just a little upset to realize how accurately the amiable cook had interpreted her feelings for both Guy and Jared.

Like it or not, and try as she had to deny her feelings, Kathy was still attracted to Jared. What woman wouldn't be? He was handsome, intelligent, strong, wealthy—everything most women could want in a man. But Kathy had already settled that matter. With all his attributes, he lacked the one thing she required in a husband—a genuine commitment to Christ. Without that, Jared Jarrett was a pauper.

And Guy . . . Oatie was right about that, too. Guy had probably fallen in love with her—while she regarded him as a good friend.

After lunch Kathy went poolside to read and soak up the sun. She didn't hear the glass doors slide open, or footsteps on the flagstone path.

"Restful, isn't it?" Jared spoke from directly behind her chaise lounge.

Startled, Kathy jumped, almost spilling her iced tea.

"Y-yes it is. You frightened me!" she blurted.

"Oatie said you were out here."

"I came out for some peace and quiet."

She knew the statement sounded abrupt, but Jared's presence always seemed to put her on edge. He had the uncanny knack of making her blurt unfortunate remarks to fill the electric atmosphere between them.

"Is that an indirect invitation for me to get lost and leave you alone?"

"I didn't say that!"

"Maybe you didn't have to," Jared murmured. For a moment, Kathy thought, the arrogant man sounded almost insecure. "Would you rather I leave, Kathy?"

She refused to look at him. Her hand trembled as she took a sip of tea. "Not if you'd prefer to stay."

Jared sighed with impatience. "It's not what *I* prefer. I just wanted to see you a moment to tell you we appreciate what you're doing for Margot, and to . . . apologize to you for this morning."

Kathy almost blurted that she hoped he'd had the good sense to apologize to Guy before he searched her out, but Jared spoke before she found the words.

"I'd like to do more than *tell* you how I feel. I'd like to take you to dinner tonight as a token. There's a Club not far away, the Old Mill Inn. They serve excellent steaks and have a very good band. Can I talk you into skipping Oatie's dinner tonight to share mine with me at the Club?"

There was a difference in Jared. How strange it seemed for him to be *asking* instead of ordering people about.

"Thanks for asking me, Jared," Kathy said carefully. "It sounds wonderful—"

"Then you'll go?" he said quickly, his gray eyes lighting.

She faced him. "No, I'm afraid not. Guy asked to see me tonight. I promised I would be available."

Jared's eyes hardened, but his voice remained soft, coaxing.

"Break the date," he ordered. "You can see Guy Armitage some other time. Any other time. I don't have many free evenings. You can think of some way to get out of it, I'm sure . . ."

A chill passed through Kathy. "Yes," she said coolly. "I could think of some way to get out of meeting Guy tonight if I wanted to—but I don't. I don't break promises—not even for you . . . *Boss*."

Jared stiffened as if he had been slapped. Kathy no longer cared if her words and attitude stung. She knew Jared couldn't ridicule her for not breaking a vow, because it was one of the few beliefs they shared.

"You're right. I shouldn't have expected you to. Perhaps some other time." Jared's voice was mild as he turned to go. He halted, his hand on the glass door. "Incidentally— you'd better see Guy while you have the chance. The roundup will take place soon. Guy Armitage is going to be a very busy person." Jared paused while the meaning was driven home. And then he was gone—finding something, or someone—to fill the evening Alana had left empty.

When Kathy and Guy saddled their horses and rode across the pasture to some of the higher hills on the ranch, Kathy felt her tension beginning to slip away.

At the crest of a hill among a clump of trees, Guy dismounted, held the reins to Kathy's horse, and helped her from the saddle. Guy's hands lingered at Kathy's slim waist when he set her on the ground and, instead of releasing her, he dropped the reins to let the horses graze and pulled her into his arms.

"Kathy . . . sweet Kathy, I love you," he whispered huskily.

She looked into Guy's face, while waves of unpleasant emotions swept over her. When Guy's lips descended to hers and his muscular arms tightened around her, Kathy shivered. Interpreting the movement to mean that she was cold, he drew her even closer. Bitter tears welled within, more for Guy than for herself. Why couldn't she feel for this good man what she felt for the bad one—the renegade—Jared?

CHAPTER 8

JARED MADE GOOD his threat.

In the days that followed, he kept Guy and all the hands so busy that by sunset each night, it was all they could do to eat the hearty meal Oatie had prepared for them, then fall exhausted into bed to rest up for the next grueling day's work.

Kathy missed Guy's cheerful company. Yet she was almost grateful that he was too busy to drop by. The inevitable question could not be asked as long as they were apart.

During the week, Bootsy Holloway invited Kathy for a meal and Kathy accepted quickly. An evening spent with vivacious Bootsy and her family would be a pleasant diversion.

Bootsy inquired about Guy as she and Kathy put away the supper dishes. Kathy was relieved when Bootsy let the subject drop and expressed interest in Margot's progress.

"Actually, she is getting along quite well," Kathy confided. "But I'm afraid there's still a long way to go."

Bootsy nodded understandingly. "Margot hasn't had an easy time of it."

"That's what Guy tells me."

"It's never easy to be the 'baby of the family.' I can vouch for that. It's even harder to live in the shadow of a big sister. I know all about that, too." Bootsy's eyes softened with the memories. "I followed behind what they call an overachiever. Sis made my life miserable by being so successful. We are close now, but back then, I'm afraid I resented her very much. Jenetia Jarrett was an exceptional girl. I've often wondered whether Margot has had the same problem. Jenny made a real mark on the world in her way—and Margot seems to be making a mark in reverse."

"I know almost nothing about Jenetia," Kathy admitted.

"I doubt that you'll learn anything about her from Jared," Bootsy mused. "Since the accident, he can't bear to talk about her. They were very, very close. Jared was piloting the airplane when it went down. As you know, Jenny was killed and Margot was injured. Jared escaped with only a few scratches. I've heard people say he blames himself. I do know he hasn't flown since."

Hours later, when Kathy drove the station wagon the short distance from the Holloway ranch to the Black Diamond, she realized that the evening spent with Bootsy and her family had been a welcome change of pace. And, in the course of conversation with her new friend, she had picked up some valuable information about the Jarrett family. She prayed a prayer of thanks as she wheeled into the gates of the Ranch.

The next evening, the night before the scheduled roundup, Jared surprised everyone by his appearance in the dining hall. As they lingered over coffee, Jared mentioned the plans to his mother, who had a week-long speaking engagement near Sioux City, Iowa, beginning the next day.

At the mention of the wild horses, Kathy noticed the look of worry that creased Mrs. Jarrett's brow.

"Can I go along on the roundup?" Margot asked.

"Absolutely not!" Her mother's answer was decisive.

"There's no need for you to go, Margot," Jared said. "I've arranged for extra help."

"But you can always use one more rider," Margot persisted.

"It's too dangerous, Margot." Mrs. Jarrett was adamant.

Margot darted an angry glance at her mother. "I'm a good rider. Nothing will happen. Give me a good reason why I shouldn't go. One good reason!"

"I don't want you to."

Margot's eyes flashed in triumph. "There! You said it yourself—and it's the only reason you have. You don't want me to! Why? Because I might have some fun?"

"Margot!" Mrs. Jarrett's voice was heavy with pain.

"On second thought, why don't you let her go, mother?" Jared urged. "You want to protect Margot, but you can't protect either of us forever. You can't shield us from all the things you'd rather we didn't experience—the risks you'd prefer we didn't take. Margot's almost fifteen. Like everyone else, she'll have to learn to make her own decisions and live with the consequences when she makes a wrong choice."

Mrs. Jarrett sadly studied her two children—the one, dark and fervent in his plea; the other, so fair and vulnerable behind the facade of rigid resistance.

"You're right," she conceded reluctantly. "Margot, it's up to you. You're free to go."

"Only if it's all right with Miss Newby," Jared insisted. "We didn't consult her to see if Margot can afford to skip a session."

"Of course," Kathy agreed.

Jared avoided her eyes. "Maybe she won't have to miss the entire session. The men and I will ride out about dawn. We probably won't locate the horses right away. Margot can study, then knock off early, it that's all right with you, Miss Newby."

Kathy winced at his cool tone, his businesslike attitude. She was no longer his "darling Kathy." She was once again "Miss Newby."

"Whatever you wish," she replied crisply, then she excused herself, carefully avoiding Jared's eyes as she left the table.

The next day Margot was dressed and ready to ride when she arrived for the session.

"Have you ever been on a roundup, Miss Newby?" she asked, as she was leaving the room.

"No . . . never."

Margot's eyes gleamed. "You ought to go. Roundups are such fun!"

Kathy smiled. "I'm sure they are but, like your mother said, dangerous. An amateur like me could get hurt."

Margot's eyes grew chilly. She shrugged. "Well . . . if you're afraid . . . stay here. I really don't care if you go along or not!"

Only then did Kathy realize that the girl's question had been a backhanded invitation. Margot, interpreting Kathy's comments as a rejection, bolted out of the house.

"Wait—Margot!" Kathy called. But it was too late.

A few minutes later, as Kathy was leaving the ell, the doorbell chimed. She opened the door to find Alana Fontaine dressed for riding in a tailored outfit, her snakeskin boots gleaming in the sunlight. Her sporty car was parked at the end of the walk, a horse trailer in tow.

"Come in," Kathy invited.

Alana stepped into the foyer. "I can't stay long. I came over to ride in the roundup. Jared hired some extra riders, but I thought I'd surprise him. Margot telephoned last night to tell me she was going so I thought we could ride out together."

"It's too bad you missed her. She left a few minutes ago."

"Already?"

Kathy nodded. "Margot hurried through the lessons this morning. She's excited about the roundup. She wanted me to go, but—"

"That's a terrific idea!" Alana exclaimed. "Why don't you?"

"I don't ride very well," Kathy admitted.

Alana wrinkled her nose. "You don't have to be an expert rider to enjoy the fun." Her eyes narrowed. "Anyway, Jared

90

tells me you've been taking moonlight rides with Guy—
that's experience enough. Go change your clothes," Alana
ordered. "I'll unload my horse and go saddle up a fat, lazy
mare for you. She'll be as gentle as a rocking chair."

"I don't know." Kathy hesitated.

Alana drew herself up to her full height and grinned at
Kathy. "I *do* know," she contradicted pertly. "I want you
to go along. Margot must have, too. It'll give us a chance to
get to know each other. There aren't many girls in these
parts. I get lonely when Jared's all tied up with his Ranch
business. I want us to be friends, Kathy."

Kathy hesitated only a moment. It seemed an attractive
proposition after all.

"You've convinced me! I'll hurry!"

Quickly Kathy changed into Margot's jeans and boots,
while Alana unloaded her Appaloosa. She was tightening
the cinch of the saddle placed on the back of a plump pinto
mare when Kathy appeared.

Alana had kept her promise. Duchess was fat and docile,
and it would have taken special effort to fall off her broad,
solid back.

"There's not a mean bone in her body," Alana said when
she handed the reins to Kathy. "Now hurry up!" Alana
called, reining her glistening horse around. "Let's catch
Margot!"

The slim redhead spurred her horse ahead. The gelding's
frosty mane and tail seemed to float in the wind as the
animal moved effortlessly. Kathy's stocky cutting horse
worked to keep up. At the pasture gate, Alana hopped down
to open it for Kathy, then mounted up again, walking her
horse to give Kathy and Duchess a chance to rest.

"My birthday is coming up next month—the middle of
August," Alana said. "Mother and I are making plans for a
big party at the Old Mill Inn. It's the nicest place in the
area." Alana adjusted her hat. "You *have* to come!"

"It sounds like fun," Kathy said.

Alana's face was hazy with happiness. "It's going to be a
very special night . . ."

"Birthdays often are."

Alana gave Kathy a secretive look. "This one will be," she promised. "Everyone worth knowing will be there—all of my friends, and Jared's friends, too. You must promise me that you and Guy will be there!"

The two young women made small talk as they walked the horses across the rolling pasture. Then, Alana reined in her horse abruptly. Duchess halted, too. The girl's green eyes were sparkling. "Don't you tell a soul what I'm going to tell you, Kathy. But I'm so happy I can't keep the news to myself any longer! Jared and I are getting engaged at my birthday party!"

Though the fact that someday Alana Fontaine would probably become Mrs. Jared Jarrett was common knowledge, the news struck Kathy with the effect of a sharp blow to the stomach.

"Congratulations!" she gasped, mustering all the enthusiasm the circumstances permitted.

"Thanks!" Alana said brightly. "Isn't it exciting? I'm so happy I could just *die*!" She hugged herself. "I want everyone to know. I can hardly keep from announcing it on every ranch in South Dakota. But, don't tell anyone, Kathy," her voice grew deadly serious. "Because if you so much as breathe a word of this and it gets out, I'm going to be furious with you!"

"Of course I won't," Kathy agreed.

Alana nodded, satisfied. "If Jared found out I already know his plans, he'd be upset that it wouldn't be a birthday surprise."

"A surprise? How did you find out?"

Alana's smile was smug. "Awhile back Jared took the Jarrett ring to the jeweler's. Mother's boutique is on the same street, and she and the jeweler's wife are quite good friends. Jared ordered the jeweler not to tell anyone that the ring was being worked on, but when his wife saw it in the safe, she *knew* what it meant. *Everyone* knows what it means. When Jared insisted the ring be ready the day before my birthday, the jeweler's wife thought mother and I should know. I'm sure Jared plans for us to get engaged at the party! I'm so happy!''

"I'm sure you are," Kathy murmured. "You've every right to be. You and Jared make a lovely couple.''

"Thank you, Kathy. It's sweet of you to say so.'' Her radiant smile was momentarily clouded by a frown. "Once we get married, everything will be fine. Right now Jared's a crank. But mama says that's normal for a man about to ask the big question. Daddy was like that, too. Once Jared and I get married . . .''

"You'll be very happy," Kathy finished the thought.

"There's Margot!" Alana cried. She nudged her horse ahead. Kathy was grateful for the concentration needed just to stay astride the bouncing mare. It afforded her no time to digest Alana's startling revelation.

In the wild horse pasture Kathy hung on the best she could, unashamedly clinging to the large saddle horse in true greenhorn fashion. Kathy gave the pinto mare free rein. Duchess fell into position when they neared the herd of broncos rushing ahead at a dizzying pace.

Jared rode at the front of the herd, his horse running neck and neck with a gray stallion that seemed to be the leader. The broncos dashed ahead, whinnying with alarm, snorting with anger, lashing and snapping at other mustangs that crowded too close.

Jared attempted to force the gray stallion to swerve, leading the thundering herd up the long draw that led to a large corral and holding pen, with thick underbrush lining both sides of the rutted ravine.

Duchess huffed with every breath. The herd surged ahead faster and faster. Mustangs lost their footing only to regain it before being trampled by those behind.

As she clung to the saddlehorn, Kathy's mind did not remain with her rigid body. It wandered to the disturbing picture of Jared and Alana at the party, their guests looking on as the Jarrett ring was placed on her delicate finger. Jared's strong hand held it there as applause and delighted laughter filled the great hall.

Had she been the only one not to recognize the significance of that priceless ring? Had she really allowed herself to be persuaded by Oatie's romantic notions, foolishly dreaming that Jared *did* feel something for her, after all. Now she knew that he did not. He had taken the Jarrett Ring to the jeweler for a purpose. Everyone else knew what it meant—that he was ready to ask Alana Fontaine to be his wife.

The memory of his burning kisses had kept her hope alive. So what if, in a moment of weakness, Jared Jarrett had kissed her? In his lifetime Jared had undoubtedly kissed hundreds of women, with no more meaning—or memory —than that he felt for her. Regardless of her love for Jared, it was now all too clear it was not returned.

Suddenly Kathy's head cleared. She was less than five feet from the stampeding mustangs! Mrs. Jarrett's warning flashed through her mind: *"It's too dangerous . . ."* Where was everybody? How had she strayed so far from the others? She was afraid to look around . . . uncertain as to how to halt Duchess's mad dash into the wild herd.

A young stallion near the edge of the pack sensed the presence of the intruder. Butting and biting his way through the rushing herd, the black yearling advanced on Duchess. Kathy saw his foam-flecked, muscled neck arched in defiance, his eyes rolled back in alarm. Her heart leapt in terror as he darted a sideways swipe at the mare's neck, his white teeth bared. Duchess whinnied in distress and swung around, almost pitching Kathy from the saddle.

"Help! Someone, help! Please!" Kathy cried. The black stallion stayed close to the mare, his nostrils flaring. He reared, pawing the air. Kathy was terrified that his flashing hooves would strike her. But instead they hit the ground with a shuddering impact.

Duchess bolted. The stallion followed, nipping at the cutting mare. Duchess stopped quickly, and spun. Kathy flew through the air. The frightened mare nickered, the reins flapping loosely around her legs as she backed away from the threatening stallion.

Kathy scrambled for the underbrush and away from the deadly hooves. She was almost to the safety of the scrubby vines and tangled bushes when the stallion backed into her, sending her sprawling. As Kathy picked herself up, another blow knocked her down. She tried to roll clear, but still another kick sent her reeling. Kathy fell back, trying vainly to protect her face with her hands. Another blow landed. Kathy sobbed with the pain. In a terrified moment she stared up to see the stallion's hooves pawing the air above her. Then, blessedly, she felt no more.

Kathy sensed rather than heard her name being called. The voice seemed distant, so far away that she was surprised when she forced her eyes open to find Jared kneeling over her. Kathy's eyes fell shut. Jared was tapping her wrists, calling her name. She tried to answer, but the only sound she could utter was a tortured moan.

"Kathy—answer me! Look at me!" Jared demanded. She fought her eyes open for a fleeting second. "We've got to get you out of here. Put your arms around me—be a good girl, Kath. Put your arms around my neck and hang on. I can't carry you like you are—you're limp as a noodle. *Hang on!*"

It was as if all the control in her muscles had evaporated. Jared picked her up, scooping her into his arms. The pain was searing as Kathy concentrated on tightening her grip around his neck. His shirt was rough beneath her fingertips.

"That's a good girl," he soothed. He carried her over the rocky ground to where his horse waited. "This ride is going to be rough for you, but I can't spare the time to carry you to the jeep. We've got to get you to the hospital right away. I'll try not to hurt you, I promise."

Jared leaned Kathy against the well-trained horse, mounted, then pulled her into his arms. She cried out with the wracking pain, then lapsed into unconsciousness.

Later, Kathy couldn't remember how Jared had gotten her onto his horse, or how he had managed the awkward ride to the holding area where the jeep was parked. She didn't even realize that it had taken all of the hands, including Margot and Alana, and every ounce of skill and strength they could muster just to control the crazed herd of mustangs.

Kathy regained consciousness for a moment as Jared tucked her gently inside the jeep and took his place behind the wheel. Kathy forced her eyes open and saw a kaleidoscope of emotions ranging over his features.

"Who caused this?" Jared asked. His voice was a whiplash of fury. "Tell me! Who did this to you?"

Kathy's head throbbed, the ache made worse by Jared's sharp questions.

"No one," she murmured, as nausea swept over her. "No one did this to me. It was an accident."

"It was no accident!" Jared's harsh response was proof her thoughts had been spoken. "I'll find out who was responsible, Kathy. I swear it. And they'll answer to me!"

Jared pressed the accelerator to the floorboard, and the jeep roared over the rutted road, twigs clawing at the windshield, branches scratching and protesting as they parted. Jared looked back at Kathy.

"Who did—" The question died on his lips when he saw her closed eyes, her small body so still and motionless, except for the swaying of the jeep.

He banged his fist on the steering wheel, knowing it was useless to fire more questions at her. She couldn't give him the answer that would point the finger of guilt at whoever wanted Kathy Newby hurt—maybe even killed.

"I'll find out," he vowed savagely. "I promise I'll find out who did this to you—if it's the last thing I do!"

CHAPTER 9

JARED PARKED THE JEEP in the rear lot of the hospital, scooped Kathy into his arms, and raced for the emergency entrance.

When Jared appeared with his limp burden, nurses set aside what they were doing and rushed for a gurney. Jared released Kathy reluctantly. His mouth was dry and metallic with the taste of fear. He stared after the cluster of technicians pushing the stretcher into the emergency room, then turned into a nearby lounge to wait.

For the first time in many years, Jared found himself praying. Praying to a God he was not at all sure even existed. A God he'd long since ceased to trust . . . Soon his prayers turned to angry curses.

It was no one's fault but his own that Kathy Newby lay hurt, maybe dying. Kathy didn't deserve it—but neither had any of the others! Three times the women Jared loved had been claimed by death. "God is taking back His own," well-meaning friends tried to comfort him at the funerals. Jared accepted their comments in mute agony, his mind silently screaming: *Why does God always take the women I have chosen to love?*

On the day of the airplane crash, his mother, knowing that he would eventually have to conquer his fear of flying, extracted a promise from him. Even as Jared agreed that someday he would fly again, he vowed to himself that he would never love again.

"But I do . . . I do," Jared whispered. He dropped his head, moaning softly as he realized the truth. He loved Kathy . . . and she was now paying for his folly.

When a registered nurse came out of the emergency room, Jared was instantly on his feet, his eyebrows raised in question. The nurse shook her head.

"I'm very sorry, Mr. Jarrett, but I can't tell you anything yet."

Jared dropped heavily into the chair, not knowing whether to pray or to curse.

"You'll have to be patient," the nurse admonished. "We're doing all we can."

He sagged with weariness. Waiting was not something Jared Jarrett did well. He was by nature an impatient man, expecting instant compliance with orders. This time he had no choice but to wait for the doctor's prognosis, just as he must also wait for Kathy's answer to the question he had asked her en route to the hospital.

Jared's thoughts returned to the events of the morning. He had seen Kathy, Margot, and Alana cresting the hill to join the roundup.

The ranch hands had been with him all morning, having ridden out from headquarters at daybreak. That narrowed the suspects. Margot or Alana. One of them had tried to hurt Kathy. But only one of the two had tried—with vicious desperation—to rid herself of Kathy in the past.

Margot!

"It had to be Margot," Jared whispered, his voice hoarse with conviction.

It was no accident. Jared had sorted out the horses himself, removing the mares in estrus from among the cutting horses in the corral so they wouldn't be ridden around the wild stallions. It was a standard procedure—and Margot

98

knew it! The muscle in Jared's jaw contracted when he realized what she had done. He clenched and unclenched his fists.

Footsteps on the hard floor of the corridor aroused Jared from his reverie. He glanced up to see Alana and Margot approaching. Fueled by his angry thoughts, Jared catapulted out of the chair and gripped Margot's arm, wordlessly propelling the startled girl down the quiet hallway, outside, and across the paved lot to the jeep. Alana watched them go— stark terror etching her lovely features.

Alana had seen Jared angry before—many times—but his previous rages had never upset her. They usually erupted and passed with the swift violence of a summer storm. But the murderous look she saw on Jared's face at the moment terrified her. More than anything, Alana wanted to run and hide, but this time she knew she couldn't escape his wrath.

Tears of confusion sprang to Margot's eyes. "Jared! What's wrong? Is she—"

Jared looked at Margot, his face white with fury. "Why did you give Kathy that mare? You know I always separate them out before a roundup. *Why?*"

"But—I didn't!"

Jared shook his head in disgust. "Don't lie to me!"

"I'm not lying!" Margot protested tearfully.

Jared was unmoved. When he spoke, his tone was cutting. "You expect me to believe you after all the lies you've told in the past to get away with your shenanigans? You expect me to believe you, *now,* when not very many days ago you stooped so low as to frame Kathy as a thief in hopes I'd fire her before mother could return? Margot, you have gall to expect me to believe you after all you did to get rid of Kathy—just like you got rid of all the others!"

"I know how it looks, Jared," she sobbed softly. "But I didn't do it. I swear I didn't."

It was as if Jared hadn't heard her. "You probably thought if you couldn't get rid of Kathy one way," he mused, "you'd do it another—even if it meant killing her."

99

Margot was crying uncontrollably now. He was past reason.

"I know I haven't been nice to Kathy—I've been awful to her. But, Jared, I don't even want Kathy to leave anymore. I never wanted her to leave enough to try to . . . kill her."

Something in Margot's tone touched Jared. She not only appeared to be telling the truth—Jared detected that she was every bit as upset about Kathy's injuries as he.

Jared sighed and ran his fingers through his hair. His voice was quieter as he proceeded to question Margot.

"Then who gave Kathy that mare?"

Margot dabbed her eyes. "I don't know, Jared," she said in a small voice. "Maybe she picked out the mare herself."

"Kathy can't even saddle up a horse! Someone else had to saddle it for her—*who*?"

"I tell you, Jared, I don't know!"

Jared gripped Margot's shoulder. The anger flickered anew in his eyes. "You rode out with her. I saw you arrive. So don't try to sit there and tell me that—"

"Jared, darling. Honey . . . Margot isn't lying to you," Alana said softly. She squirmed into Jared's arms, and tears brimmed in her eyes as she bit her lip. She trembled, burrowing against Jared. "Margot isn't lying," Alana whimpered. Tears spilled over, dampening the thin material stretched across Jared's broad chest. "I gave Kathy that horse, because I knew Duchess was lazy and gentle. It was stupid of me, I know. Being raised on a ranch, I should have known better. But, Jared . . . I just . . . didn't think why those mares weren't with the other horses."

Alana peeked at Jared's rigid features. Jared disengaged himself from Alana's embrace. Wordlessly he turned and walked toward the hospital entrance. Alana stared after him, her heart in her throat, guilt in her green eyes.

Alana skittered across the lot and caught up with Jared, shooting a warning glance over her shoulder in Margot's direction as she did. When their eyes met, Margot understood. Perfectly. She turned away, sickened, when she heard Alana expressing sorrow, claiming it was an accident.

"She's going to be all right, isn't she, darling?" Alana asked as Jared held the hospital door open and she quickly stepped inside.

"I don't know," Jared said. "I just don't know."

In the jeep fresh tears stung in Margot's eyes as she stared at her hands. One by one the bitter tears rolled down her cheeks. Savagely she swiped them away.

Margot had never seen her brother so angry. Or so helpless. She wanted to reach out to him, to comfort him, but she didn't know what to do or what to say, and she knew she couldn't bear to seek him out in Alana's presence.

Quite some time later, Alana, looking much relieved, left the hospital, without so much as casting Margot a backward glance. Only after Alana backed her car from the parking lot and sped away did Margot leave the jeep and walk slowly into the hospital.

"She's not out of the emergency room yet?" Margot asked. Only minutes had passed. It seemed like an eternity.

"Not yet," Jared replied.

Margot slipped into the chair next to his. The waiting room was so quiet that the clock on the wall above them ticked audibly.

"I wanted Kathy to leave, Jared," Margot confessed. "I did everything I could think of to make it happen. Now that we may lose her, I know how much I want her to stay. She's a wonderful person." Margot faced Jared, searching his face, his eyes. "You care for her, don't you, Jared?"

He tensed at her words. Slowly he raised his eyes to Margot's and nodded curtly. "Of course I care for her." He took a quick breath and glanced away before he spoke. "I care about all our . . . employees."

"I mean *really* care for her. You love her, don't you?"

"No. No, I don't!" The denial was spoken quickly—too quickly to be fully believed.

Margot said softly. "You *do* love her, Jared. I can tell!"

When he said nothing, Margot knew she had been right all along. She had noticed the way Jared had looked at

Kathy when Kathy wasn't aware of his eyes on her. Margot had seen the way Jared turned on Guy so unfairly whenever Kathy was involved. Margot had noticed Oatie's knowing smiles. And her mother's fond gazes.

It was plain to everyone, Margot decided, that Jared loved Kathy. If it was that plain to all of them at the Ranch, Alana certainly couldn't be ignorant of Jared's feelings. With that realization, Alana would have plenty of reason to remove Kathy from the running and firm up her own precarious position with Jared.

Alana's warning glance confirmed what Margot had only suspected. It was no accident. Alana couldn't fool her as she had Jared with her easy tears and trembling words of self-recrimination. Jared believed Alana only because he wanted to believe her.

The hinges on the emergency room door squeaked as a nurse held them wide for the attendants to wheel out the stretcher. Jared and Margot crossed the hall as the doctor came out, untying his face mask.

"Is she—" Margot began.

"She's going to be fine," the doctor smiled. "She took a nasty bump on the head and picked up some cuts and bruises. We'll keep her overnight for observation. If all goes well, we can release her in the morning. A few days of rest, and she'll be good as new."

"Thank God," Margot breathed. "Kathy's going to be all right!"

A wide grin split Jared's face. "I heard the man, pet," he said and slipped his arm around Margot, giving her a squeeze.

Margot was overwhelmed by unfamiliar feelings of joy. She was so happy that she felt like doing cartwheels down the corridors! Over the weeks Margot had felt herself changing, even as she resisted the process. The bothersome new attitudes seemed as if someone else were taking control of her life. Instead of fighting, she had yielded, and now felt incredibly free!

Margot searched Jared's face. She wondered if he had

102

noticed the difference. Or if he had struggled with the same strange feelings. If he had, Margot knew he would have resisted every bit as much as she. Resisted in vain, Margot thought. Jared had as much as admitted he loved Katherine Newby.

Reality sent a sudden chill through Margot. Jared's vague admission meant nothing! Her brother was the kind of man who was quite capable of secretly loving Kathy—and marrying Alana anyway!

Jared didn't leave Kathy's side once the nurses settled her in a private room. As she slept, sedated, Jared kept vigil in a chair beside her bed. Toward evening, when Guy arrived to collect Margot and see Kathy for a few minutes, Jared left the room to afford them privacy.

Even as Jared watched Guy take his place beside Kathy's bed while she slept, and even when Guy took her hand as if it were quite naturally his to hold, Jared didn't feel the smarting sting of jealousy that had consumed him in past weeks. Guy Armitage loved Kathy. That was a fact.

For once the knowledge didn't bring unreasonable anger to Jared's heart. Kathy deserved a man like Guy. He was good. Kind. Decent. Guy would never cause Kathy heartache or bring her grief.

Even though Jared knew that his kiss had awakened a passion in Kathy that rivaled his own, he also knew it was foolishness to dream that anything could come of his feelings for her. He could only end up breaking her heart.

Jared knew it was time to remedy the situation before he lost the best foreman the Black Diamond Ranch had ever had. And before he made a complete fool of himself in the bargain.

So what if he loved Kathy? In the past he had loved, lost, and lived to go on. He would get over it this time, too. The accident had been like a warning. He loved Kathy—enough to encourage her to fall in love with another man—one who was worthy of her.

When Jared stepped into the hallway, Guy leaned over Kathy's still form.

"Kathy," Guy called softly. She tossed in her sleep, the sedative clouding her senses. "Kathy!"

At the sound of her name, she tried to open her eyes. "Mmmmm . . . ," she sighed. Guy called her name again and Kathy's eyelids flickered open, her gaze focusing on Guy's face before her lids drooped shut again.

Kathy and Guy had looked at each other for only a moment, but a moment was all it took for Guy to recognize the truth. Guy saw the fleeting disappointment mirrored in Kathy's blue eyes when she discovered it was he and not Jared who had awakened her. The look was there for only a second, before the gentle smile reserved for a good friend, but not given to a lover, radiated up at him.

Tenderly Guy tucked the sheet under Kathy's chin, touched her cheek, then brushed a kiss across her smooth brow. No matter what happened, he would always cherish that friendship. For that, Guy was grateful.

"She's all yours, Jared," Guy said. The meaning was lost on Jared as Guy walked past him and went to find Margot for the trip back to the Ranch.

When Jared brought Kathy home the next morning, Mrs. Otis clucked like a mother hen over her favorite chick. Guy stopped by for a few minutes to tease Kathy. "Maybe you and Margot should 'make a swap.' You could teach her reading and 'rithmetic. And she could teach you *riding*."

"Nut!" Kathy laughed softly. "Speaking of Margot— where is she?"

"Beats me," Guy said. "I haven't seen her since I brought her back last night. Have you, Boss?"

"No, Guy, but I'll go look for her. You stay here with Kathy."

It was spoken like an order—and accepted as such. Both Guy and Kathy stared after Jared, perplexed, and exchanged a questioning glance. Before, Jared had always seemed to resent their sharing a few minutes of casual conversation.

How unusual to have him actually *ordering* Guy to remain with her!

"I thought Margot might be here along with everyone else," Kathy said.

"It doesn't surprise me," Guy explained. "We talked on the way home. I think she's . . . ashamed to face you."

"Ashamed?" Kathy asked. "Why? Guy, she shouldn't be!"

"I know that. You know it. Margot doesn't see it that way. After making such a pest of herself, she's afraid you'll think she's a phony if she's friendly now."

"The poor child. Maybe we'll get a chance to talk later."

"I hope so," Guy said. "Margot really needs someone. She was so desperate last night that, if Mrs. Jarrett hadn't been away, I think Margot would have looked up her mother."

"It was *my* fault for going along."

"No, Kath, it was *not* your fault."

Before Guy could elaborate, Jared and Alana walked into Kathy's room, hand-in-hand. Oatie followed with an arrangement the florist had just delivered.

"Now don't stay too long," Mrs. Otis ordered sharply, scarcely bothering to mask her feelings for Alana. "Kathy's still not well."

Alana seated herself on the edge of Kathy's bed and plumped the pillow. "You look so awful, dear," she purred, "and it's all my fault for being so addle-brained as to give you that horse. Can you ever forgive me?" Alana didn't wait for a reply. "Poor, poor Kathy. The bruises . . ." She shuddered as she touched Kathy's forehead. "It must break your heart to look this way. It almost hurts to look at you."

Guy cleared his throat. "I think Kathy looks wonderful," he said in a hearty voice. "Having her alive makes her more beautiful than ever."

"Right!" Jared agreed quickly. Kathy had not looked in a mirror since the accident. She supposed she *did* look a fright.

Alana pouted flirtily. "You two! Just like men. That wasn't what I meant at all, and you know it. Of course it's wonderful that Kathy's alive and is going to be just fine. Tell me, love, how do you like the flowers Jared and I ordered for you? I hope you like yellow roses. They're my favorites!"

"They're lovely. It was very thoughtful."

Kathy's head began to throb. Guy, sensitive to her fatigue, spoke up. "I think we'd better leave Kathy alone so she can rest, before Oatie runs us off with a rolling pin."

"Good idea!" Jared said, and seemed relieved that the visit was coming to an end.

"Concentrate on getting well," Alana ordered as she touched her cheek to Kathy's. "Remember! My birthday party is coming up soon. We'll expect you to be feeling fit by then. Won't we, Jared?"

He smiled lazily, his thoughts far away. "Anything you say, pet," he agreed.

Jared and Alana left together, and Guy stayed behind only long enough to promise Kathy he would be back that evening. She nodded. Before Guy left the room, Kathy had closed her eyes and was fast asleep.

CHAPTER 10

A CREAKING SOUND IN the hallway outside Kathy's door awakened her. She opened her eyes, but saw nothing. When she heard the creak again, she found Margot Jarrett standing at the door.

Kathy's heart wrenched at the forlorn look on Margot's face. Kathy wondered how long the girl had been standing there, waiting for her to wake up, trying to muster courage to enter the room.

"Margot—come in," Kathy called cheerfully. "I was hoping you'd come see me."

Margot stepped in and closed the door quickly behind her. "I've got to talk to you, Kathy."

"What's wrong, Margot?" Kathy pushed herself to a sitting position, wincing as she did. Margot's face was splotched with anger. "What is it?"

"Ohhhhhh. . . ." Margot groaned through clenched teeth and dropped to the edge of the bed. "I hate Alana! I *hate* her!"

"Margot!" Kathy was shocked by the vehemence of her words.

"It's true! She makes me positively sick!" After Margot's initial outburst, unshed tears shone in her eyes. "To think I wanted to be just like her," Margot whispered. "She used me, Kathy. All I was to her was a—a puppet. I not only let her use me—I helped her do it! She never cared about me. All she cares about is herself and what she wants. Almost every crummy thing that's happened here traces back to her. It's her fault you got hurt yesterday."

"Margot, honey, don't say things like that," Kathy murmured.

"It's true!" Margot said, her eyes flashing. "Jared knew it was no accident and he blamed me, because I've been pretty, well . . . hateful to you. Jared was yelling at me when Alana stepped in and told him what happened. She convinced Jared that it was a foolish mistake on her part. He believed her because he wants to. Alana's acting like she feels terrible that you're hurt, but if Alana's sorry about anything, it's only that you weren't hurt even worse!"

"Calm down, Margot," Kathy begged. "You're too worked up about all this. Don't say things you might later regret. Sometimes when we're upset, we think awful things about other people—things we later learn weren't true at all." She sighed, "And sometimes we shouldn't even discuss what we know for certain to be a fact, because some things are much better left unsaid."

Margot wiped at her eyes with the back of her hand. "I don't know who I hate worse—her or me. When I think of the things I did to get her to approve of me, Kathy . . . *I could just die*!"

In a torrent of words, Margot unburdened her heart. Choking on tears, she spilled out her unhappy story.

"After the accident I missed so much school that I was way behind. I lost a year. School was never easy for me; not like it was for Jared. Or . . . for Jenny. Every teacher said to me the first day: 'Oh, you're Jenetia Jarrett's little sister!'" Margot's voice changed pitch. Her eyes ached with remembered hurts. "Then they'd tell me what a genius Jen was. How smart. How talented. How popular. How wonderful. Then they'd tell me that they were expecting good things from me, too.'' She angrily flung her long hair away from her troubled face. ''Maybe those teachers expected good things—but that's not what they got! They learned fast that I'm not Jenny! I could never live up to the wonderful Jarrett name!''

''It must have hurt very much,'' Kathy said softly.

''Alana wanted me to go East. She said I'd meet cultured people there—not people like the local ranch families. I know now that Alana wanted me out of her way, so she'd have Jared all to herself. I wanted to go where no one knew my family, where no one cared who I was or what I did.'' Margot's voice dropped low. Her shoulders heaved. When she looked at Kathy, tears coursed down her cheeks. ''Kathy, you've no idea how many times I wished that *I* had died in the crash instead of Jenny. She could've been such a comfort to mother and Jared. Instead, they got . . . stuck with me.''

''Your mother and brother love you for the person you are, honey. If your mother wants you to do anything with your life, Margot, it's to develop the talents God has given *you,* to become the person the Lord intends *you* to be. She doesn't want a replacement for Jenny. God made you and He loves you—*just as you are!* We all love you, not for who or what you think we'd like you to be, but because you are *you.*''

''I tried to be more like Jenny, to make mother happy, but it didn't work. I studied hard in school, but still I failed. Some teachers got mad and said I wasn't trying. But, Kathy, I *was* trying. I swear I was. And—''

''And after they had accused you often enough . . . you *quit* trying, right?''

Margot nodded. ''How did you know?''

''I've seen it before,'' Kathy explained. ''It's not easy to keep working when no one appreciates your efforts.''

''I wanted mom to be able to be proud of me, like she was of Jenny. I was so unhappy, and mother has been, too. I wanted to force her to let me go away. When I think of how I've treated her—I'm so ashamed . . .''

109

"We all make mistakes. I went through that same sort of thing when I was about your age. I have no doubt there were times when I was growing up that I gave my mother cause to worry. But mother and I made it through those trying years and we became very good friends. You and your mother will, too."

"I doubt that," she said after a moment's hesitation. "Not after all the ugly things I've done. Some of them were pretty unforgivable."

"You underestimate your mother, Margot. In her heart, I'm sure, she has already forgiven you, just as I forgave the unpleasantness between us, and would hope that you'd find it in yourself to forgive me any pain or unhappiness I've caused you. People can't store up old hurts like little trinkets in a treasure chest to be brought out regularly, examined, and remembered. We need to forgive others, Margot, then forget the hurts as if they'd never happened."

"You forgave me? Even about the Jarrett ring?"

Kathy nodded. "It wasn't easy, because I was hurt and very angry. I was sad that you disliked me so much that you'd try to ruin my name to get rid of me. But a person with problems often acts hastily. And I knew you were hurting for some reason, Margot, so I forgave you. Not only that—I prayed for you."

"You prayed for *me*?"

"Every day," Kathy said. "Several of us have been praying that you'd let Jesus Christ come into your heart and take away your hurt and bitterness. I know that your mother prays for that, too. Nothing would make her happier."

"I wish I could be as sure as you are that mother can—has—forgiven me," Margot sighed.

"You can be sure. Get my Bible from the dresser. I'll find you proof—if proof is what you want."

Margot picked up the new Bible that replaced the old one that had been destroyed in the fire at Miss Atwood's Academy. Kathy thumbed quickly through the pages, finding the familiar passage.

110

"Here." She pointed a finger at the selected chapter. "Read this, Margot. My eyes are tired."

Margot, who had stubbornly refused to read for Kathy in study sessions, accepted the book with a frightened glance. Frowning, she gazed at the page. In a halting voice Margot began, stumbling over words, as the letters transposed before her eyes. Kathy, from memory, gently prompted her with the correct words. Margot's eyes were misty when she closed Kathy's Bible in her lap. Kathy smiled at her.

"How happy the Father was when his prodigal son returned to him," she whispered. "No happier, Margot, than your mother will be when she comes home and learns that her daughter has returned to her."

"Oh, Kathy!" Margot flung herself into the older girl's arms. "I was so afraid that mother wouldn't be able to forgive me. Now I can't wait to see her!"

Margot was radiant when she left Kathy's room. Kathy flipped the Bible open to the passage Margot had struggled so hard to read and comprehend. Like a miracle, the last piece of the puzzle fell into place.

Kathy knew then that Margot's aversion to reading wasn't just a stronghold of defiance. Margot refused to read aloud, not out of stubbornness, but because she dreaded the ridicule and mocking laughter that might follow as the letters played tricks before her eyes.

Margot wasn't the stupid girl she thought she was. Like thousands of other people, she had been living with *dyslexia,* undoubtedly aggravated by the trauma of the accident. Part of Margot's problems were of her own making, but the underlying problem was a learning disability Margot couldn't help. After a long period of failure, Margot would gain confidence as she learned, once again, what it was like to succeed.

Within a few days, Kathy's bruises had faded to the point that a light dusting of face power covered them. Soon she felt well enough to begin tutoring again. Already she saw dramatic changes in the girl's attitude. Margot sought her out during her free time, and Kathy's days were full and happy as she spent them with Margot, seeing as much of the young girl as she saw little of Jared. Since the day he had brought her home from the hospital, Jared Jarrett had been avoiding her.

Kathy was resting after lunch when Margot knocked on her door and entered, an impish smile on her face.

"I came in to inform you that I'm playing hooky tomorrow. So can you—if you want."

Kathy laughed. "After the study sessions we've put in recently, it sounds good to me. Is there something special about tomorrow?"

"Special is right," Margot said. "We're going to the bucking horse auction."

"The what?" Kathy asked.

"You know, the wild horse auction. Jared and the hands have the broncos separated out and ready to ship to the auction to be sold. Guy told me I could ride in the semi with him. He says there's plenty of room for you, too. Please go, Kathy! It'd be so much fun."

"It sounds interesting," she admitted. "Is it far?"

"Not too far," Margot said. "There are wild horse auctions all over the West. Sometimes we take our horses as far away as the other side of Wyoming, but this sale is in easy driving distance. Jared has some business to take care of first, so he's driving to the auction later."

"What time do we leave?"

"Before sunup," Margot said.

Kathy groaned and covered her face with a pillow. Margot laughed.

It was still dark when Kathy and Margot left the house the next morning. The diesel engine in the tractor cab that pulled the long, stock rig thrummed in the still morning air as Guy and the other hands loaded the broncos at the holding pen. Then Guy drove the rig up the bouncing, rutted trail to the headquarters and parked, waiting for Kathy and Margot to climb up.

"Ready to go?" he asked.

"More than ready!" Margot said.

Guy let out the clutch and the powerful motor roared as the Jarrett rig rolled forward, the yellow beams of the headlights casting a wide glow over the rocky driveway. The wild horses in the long steel trailer whinnied loudly, and the trailer shook with dull thuds as the fighting buckers thrashed violently.

"We'll quiet 'em down when I get out on the highway," Guy said, holding the steering wheel tight against the rocking sway of the rig.

Carefully Guy snaked the long rig on the highway, deserted at the predawn hour. He picked up speed, shifting through gear after gear as the truck growled low, going faster and faster. Kathy was terrified that they would jackknife, as she felt the tension snap through the length of the vehicle. The lurching and whinnying reached a crescendo pitch, and the fighting animals, who now had to fight for their footing, quieted down and settled in for the ride.

Guy grinned. "They do it every time. We settle 'em down right off the bat."

The rest of the ride through the early morning haze went by peacefully as they crossed the Badlands, headed West.

When they neared the bucking horse auction grounds, Kathy felt the mounting excitement. Other rigs, much like the Jarrett semi, were lined up, waiting their turns to unload livestock. Guy fell in line.

"You girls don't have to wait for me. Go in and grab us some good seats in the bleachers. And save one for Jared. He should be along directly."

Kathy was stiff from the long ride. She and Margot walked to the large auction building and climbed the bleachers that were fast filling with ranchers, local people as well as well-dressed rodeo contractors, grouped in small clusters at ringside.

"Guy—over here!" Margot cried, waving to the tall foreman when he appeared much later after unloading the horses and attending to the business of hiring riders to show the Jarrett livestock in the arena.

"Jared should be here soon," Guy said when he took the

seat beside Margot and the auctioneer stepped up to the podium and passed a sheaf of papers to the man clerking the sale. "There's no hurry," Guy added. "They won't sell our stock for a long time."

The auctioneer adjusted his ten-gallon hat and cleared his throat as he picked up the microphone and smiled at the people gathered in the bleachers.

"Welcome, folks," his voice echoed over the public address system. "We've got lots of prime horseflesh to offer today—and some fine young rodeo riders who'll show you just what these buckers can do. We want to thank you all for coming, and we hope this will be the best sale ever." He glanced at the counter. "Our first lot in chute number one is a horse from the Circle K Spread at Tioga, North Dakota."

A cowboy in a bright red plaid shirt, with a kerchief around his neck, gingerly straddled a chocolate brown horse in the first chute. He dropped lightly into the saddle. When he got a good grip, he nodded tensely at the chute man. At the rider's signal, the man threw the gate open.

"Let 'er buck, boys!" the auctioneer cried. Then he began his chant.

The chute handler scrambled out of the way as the stocky horse twisted from the narrow chute, spun in a circle, then cleared the boards. The horse lunged; his nose dipped to the dusty ground as his hind legs kicked for the sky. Saddle leather squealed with stress. The rider tried to anticipate the bronco's movements, raking his spurs across the mustang's withers to make the horse buck even harder.

The auctioneer chanted numbers in a rhythmic tongue, his words rolling smoothly, from one to another. The auctioneer nodded each time he took a bid and, with his baton, urged the bidders even higher.

"Going once . . . going twice . . . going three times—and sold!" he cried.

The rider slipped from the bucker's back, hitting the ground with a rolling gait as he reached out to be pulled onto the pick up man's mount.

"It's almost as exciting as a real rodeo, isn't it?" Jared

said, when he slipped into the vacant seat beside Kathy.

"I've never been to anything like this before. It's fascinating!"

"By the time you see all the horses, you'll be tired of it. The horse that's going to sell right now won't bring a very good price." Jared settled back in the bleacher seat and crossed his long legs. Kathy regarded him with interest.

"How do you know already?"

"That horse isn't acting up in the chute. He's young enough to be broken for a riding horse, so he'll probably sell low. The rodeo contractors don't want horses who won't buck. Jarrett buckers are almost never sold to be broken for riding horses."

"We should do well," Guy said, leaning across to speak to Jared. "The buyers seem in a mood for fresh horses. Wait until they see what we've got!"

"Just what I was thinking," Jared replied.

"How much longer before our stock sells?" Margot asked Guy.

"Not much longer," he answered. "I recognized some of these horses from the load a few trucks ahead of us."

Within another half-hour, the auctioneer paused briefly between ranchers' lots, then began detailing the merits of the Black Diamond Ranch bucking stock. Jared appeared casual throughout his comments, but Kathy knew he couldn't help being pleased by the praise of the auctioneer for the Jarrett broncos. The auctioneer listed the colorful names of several famous rodeo buckers raised on the Black Diamond, among them one spirited horse that had achieved so much prominence that a monument was erected in his honor when he died.

"Look at that mustang fight," Guy said, whistling under his breath when the first Jarrett bucker was forced into a chute.

The horse shrilled angrily, spun around, snapping as it kicked powerfully. The chute man didn't wait for the rider's customary nod. He didn't want to chance that the thrashing horse would crush the rider against the planks in the chute,

115

breaking the rider's leg. The handler flung the gate open the instant the rider hit the saddle.

The bay horse came out of the chute snorting like a dragon, bucking high. The mustang landed stiff-legged, jarring the rider with neck-snapping impact. The horse flew into action again, and the rider hung on a few more seconds before he and the bucker parted ways. The cowboy landed in the dust, grinned good-naturedly, stood up, smacked the dust off his jeans then loped for the rungs and climbed out of the arena.

Contractors bid wildly on the animal, snapping fingers, waving, shouting as they vied for the horse. A contractor from Colorado was the successful bidder.

The next horse bucked out of the chute as hard as the first. A third horse was brought out. Then a fourth. All the horses from the Black Diamond were such wily buckers that few of the riders stayed on until the auctioneer's hammer fell.

The auctioneer was about to announce the next number when a stock handler cut across the arena, stepped up to the auction platform, and handed the auctioneer a slip of paper. He glanced at the note, then his eyes scanned the audience.

"Paging Jared Jarrett. Jared Jarrett, report to the chute area at once," he announced.

As Jared rose, Guy started up. "Do you want me to go with you, Boss?"

"No need. It's probably nothing," Jared dismissed. "Perhaps some confusion over a bill of sale. Stay here and keep track of what the horses bring, so I can tally the totals and make sure they match up with the master sheet when we settle accounts after the sale." Jared handed Guy the small leather notebook where he'd been noting numbers and names.

When three more horses sold, Guy grew concerned. "Maybe I'd better go back and see what's keeping the Boss."

"Jared probably got sidetracked talking to another rancher," Margot said.

"Probably," Guy agreed.

"Now, for another horse from the famous Jarrett line," the auctioneer cried. "A black stallion in chute number five!"

Every eye was drawn to chute five. Startled, Kathy recognized the vicious black maverick that had attacked Duchess in the pasture! The well-dressed rider climbed the rungs to the top of the chute, swung up, then poised over the thrashing horse.

"No—*Jared! No!*"

Margot's scream of recognition pierced the arena. Margot looked at Kathy, horrified. She threw herself into Kathy's arms, unable to look. Guy, who'd seen Mr. Jarrett killed in the same arena, stared, dazed, his face growing pale beneath his deep tan.

"He can't—he shouldn't—" Guy whispered.

Jared jumped, straddling the stallion at the same instant he yelled for the chute man to flip the gate. Kathy didn't want to watch, but she was helpless to look away. A silent prayer moved on her lips. She stared, wide-eyed, even though she feared any instant Jared would be thrown, trampled, and killed by the horse that was loco with rage.

The black stallion snorted like a demon, twisted— catlike—then lashed around to bare his teeth at the irksome pest on his back. He landed stiff-legged, only to fly again into the air, whirling in a frenzy of movement.

Jared raked the stallion mercilessly. A minute later Kathy could see that Jared was tiring, but his iron grip held. When the auctioneer's hammer fell after the wild bidding, Jared was still astride.

"Get 'im, boys," the auctioneer ordered.

The pick up men timed their movements to the bronco's. One of the riders diverted the crazed stallion's attention, while the other darted in. Jared released his grip and slid across onto the back of the skittish quarter horse. Jared retrieved his hat which had been knocked off during the ride and made his way up to the bleachers where Guy, Kathy, and Margot were seated.

117

Margot gave him a scowl as he drew near. "Jared Jarrett," her eyes narrowed with anger. "I'm so relieved you're safe that I feel like killing you myself! How could you do that? You know mother never wanted anyone from the Ranch to ride the buckers again! When daddy died, you promised mother . . ."

"No, he didn't promise," Guy said quietly.

"Guy's right, Margot. Mother wanted me to promise her I'd never ride a bronco again, but I wouldn't do it. If you'll remember, pet," Jared said, chucking Margot under the chin, "I don't make promises if I think sometime I might be required to break them. The hired rider for that horse backed out on us; I didn't have time to hire another rider, so I rode the horse myself."

Kathy felt giddy with relief. "You could have been hurt," she scolded, "even killed."

Jared turned his gaze on her. "You would have cared, Miss Newby?" he asked lightly, almost mockingly. Kathy felt her face burn under his probing gaze. When she spoke again, she made sure her voice was as detached as his.

"Of course I would have cared," Kathy said crisply. "I'd have cared about *anyone* getting hurt."

"Yes," Jared agreed. "*You would* care about . . . *anyone.*" Kathy couldn't tell if he meant the remark as a compliment or a rebuke.

"I think I'll head the rig back to the Ranch," Guy said after the Jarrett stock was sold. "I've seen enough to suit me."

"I'll go with you, Guy," Margot said. She was on her feet instantly. Kathy started to follow, but Margot firmly and gently pushed her back in the bleacher seat. "You look terribly tired, Kathy. I think you'd be much more comfortable riding in the car than you would bouncing around in the rig." Margot appealed to Jared. "Why don't you take Kathy with you, Jared?"

Kathy glared at Margot, ready to protest, but Margot smiled innocently. Kathy fumed. Margot was as open in her matchmaking as Oatie! She looked to Guy to intervene, but

Guy's smile was careful, his eyes revealing nothing.

"Good idea, Margot," Guy said. "Not that we wouldn't enjoy your company, Kathy, but you *would* be better off with Jared." Margot looked smug.

"Then it seems it's settled, doesn't it?" Jared asked coolly. "Since they're determined we return to the Ranch together, come along, Miss Newby. But I'm warning you now, I don't take kindly to back-seat drivers even if they're sitting in the front seat beside me."

Kathy didn't know if he were serious or joking, but as Guy and Margot had disappeared out a side door, she had no choice other than following Jared. She had to hurry to keep up with him as he strode through the auction building to the main office to settle up the account.

"Let's go," he said shortly, tucking the check for the load of horses into the inner pocket of his jacket. Kathy sensed that he was every bit as displeased at having her with him as she was unhappy about being forced into his company.

Kathy felt terribly self-conscious when Jared unlocked the door on the passenger side of his Jaguar and helped her into the expensive car that still held the tantalizing aroma of Alana Fontaine's perfume. She stared at her hands and a dry lump lodged in her throat.

What on earth would she and Jared find to talk about on the long ride back? A fresh wave of irritation at Margot and Guy washed over her. She couldn't believe that, after the way Jared had avoided her in the past few days, they had had the nerve to hand her over into his care like an excess piece of baggage!

CHAPTER 11

JARED JARRETT HAD no trouble finding a topic of conversation on the ride home. He gave Kathy a pointed look when he settled into the driver's seat and laughed with bitter amusement.

"I'm surprised at Guy—shoving us together like this," Jared announced as he started the engine. Kathy's face burned with embarrassment. "Guy's quite in love with you. But, of course, you know that."

He shifted gears and backed from the parking lot. He seemed to be waiting for Kathy to say something. When she didn't respond, he continued. "Guy Armitage is a very decent fellow."

"He's a wonderful person," Kathy agreed.

"I can tell Guy wants to marry you, Miss Newby." Jared gave Kathy an appraising glance. "I knew we'd lose him someday. You'll be happy together, but we're going to miss Guy."

Kathy didn't care for the way the conversation was going. She liked even less the fact that Jared was poking his nose into her private life, and Guy's. But as long as Guy and Jared had been good friends, she suspected Jared felt he had the right. Or perhaps it was his need to dominate and control. Nevertheless, Kathy decided to clear up the matter right away, and, if necessary, to suggest that he mind his own business. Not hers.

"Guy *is* wonderful," Kathy said carefully. "I like him very much. But you're wrong in thinking you'll be losing Guy and that we've been making . . . plans." She took a deep breath. "I like Guy, but I don't love him."

Jared seemed shocked "Do you love someone else?" He asked quickly, as if it had never occurred to him until that very moment that she might have left someone behind. Someone who was waiting for her in Missouri.

Kathy thought of her feelings for Jared . . .

"No, of course not!" she hotly denied.

Jared gave Kathy a patient look. "Then don't let 'love' get in the way of happiness," he suggested. "So what if you don't 'love' Guy? Let his love be enough for now. People from other cultures do exactly that. They learn to love *after* marriage, not *before*."

"I couldn't!" Kathy wanted no further part of the discussion, but found herself helpless to keep silent. "I'd rather remain single forever than even consider marrying a man I didn't love with all my heart!"

Jared gave her a wry glance. "Then you really *are* a fool," he said, his voice bitter.

"It seems to me we're back at square one," Kathy observed dryly. "The night I arrived at the Black Diamond you called me a fool—several times. After I made headway with Margot, you called me a miracle worker. A genius. Today I have been demoted."

"Don't be so touchy!"

Kathy flared. "Then don't be so nosy!" Her eyes sparked.

"I'm not being nosy! I happen to prefer that things run smoothly on the Black Diamond. That includes the lives of *my employees*. It's obvious to everyone how Guy feels about you." Jared's voice softened. "You can't fault me for trying to help things along a bit and get two nice people together. I apologize if you view it as meddling in your love life." Jared smiled boyishly. Kathy felt her anger melting away. "Many people wed for practical reasons and have very good marriages, without letting a foolish emotion like love get in their way."

"What about you?" Kathy asked boldly. "Don't you love Alana Fontaine?"

Jared was amused by the thought. "Of course not," he said, unashamed of the fact. Defensively he met Kathy's eyes. "Don't be such a child! Not everyone values love as you do." Jared's voice was mocking. He drove a long while in silence. Kathy could not say anything, and Jared chose not to. "I can tell you're shocked," he said finally. "But there's so sense lying about it. I don't love Alana and she knows it. I will never love again. *Never*!"

"Never?" Kathy murmured the question.

Jared glanced at her. "Never *again.*" He stared straight ahead at the highway as the car ate up the miles. "For you, Miss Newby, perhaps love means happily-ever-after. For me, love means only pain and loss."

"Then you *have* loved?"

"Ahhh, yes," Jared breathed. "Long ago when I was young and foolish, I loved. Repeatedly, even." His mouth twisted into a rueful smile. "As you know, some people learn faster than others. When it came to love, I was not at the head of the class. However, I eventually learned my lesson."

Even though Kathy was shocked, she grew sympathetic as Jared emptied his heart of years of stored hurts.

"Yes, I have loved. Good girls. Wonderful girls. *Christian* women." The word was used in derision. "It's true that the good die young. So, that almost guarantees that Alana and I shall live to a ripe old age together. Perhaps our years won't be happy ones, but I have no doubt that they'll be interesting ones. No, I don't love Alana, but I think we suit each other, deserve each other. I can tolerate her behavior, as she'll have to put up with mine. Alana's not the 'good' girl mother would have for me, but I've loved quite enough 'good' girls in my life, only to lose them.'' Behind Jared's eyes a war raged quietly as he searched Kathy's face. ''My love is a curse. It's like issuing an invitation, or daring God to strike my lover down in one bloody way or another!''

''Jared!''

Kathy was incredulous at the twisted logic and wrath behind his arguments. She knew that he scoffed at his mother's faith, but until that moment, Kathy had no idea how deep, how bitter his feelings ran. Jared Jarrett not only resented God, Jared despised Him . . .

Jared recognized the look in Kathy's eyes. He laughed defensively.

''You and mother are a good pair. Following all the commandments. Turning the other cheek. Praying for guidance. Looking for good in everyone. Loving your enemies even as they hate you. To you and mother, God is the loving Father of the New Testament. But to me? He has only revealed Himself to me as the bloodthirsty, punishing Patriarch of the Old.''

''You can't mean that,'' Kathy whispered.

Jared gave her a flat look. ''I not only *can* mean it; I *do* mean it. All God has ever done for me is give me a rough time. You may swear He runs your life well. I swear I can handle my life a lot better. And save your Christian witnessing for some other poor soul. I've heard quite enough of that malarky in my lifetime, more often than not, out of the mouths of some of the worst *hypocrites* to be found.''

Kathy wanted to explain to Jared that you don't judge Christ, or Christianity, by the behavior of Christian people, because people aren't perfect. She wanted desperately to make him understand that just because a person is a Christian doesn't mean that person will never fall victim to a weak human nature, rebelling against the will of God.

Before Kathy could formulate her beliefs, the jumbled feelings that Jared had locked away in his hardened heart for years gushed forth. Shock gave way to pity as Kathy listened to the litany of hurt. She could almost understand how he could feel driven to believe as he did.

"My first girl friend, Leila, was my high-school sweetheart," he began. "We were almost inseparable. Everyone assumed we'd get married. When I went off to the University of South Dakota, Lee said she'd wait for me. She was the perfect Christian girl, from a good family. The pastor gave Leila a good Christian burial, after she bled to death on the makeshift operating table of a backstreet abortionist in Minneapolis,"

"No . . ." Kathy whispered.

Jared's eyes were hollow and dull with the memory.

"The baby wasn't mine—if that's what you're thinking. As the Good Book would say . . . *I had not known her.*"

"I'm so sorry," she murmured.

"Like a trusting fool I loved again—a girl I met my senior year at the university. She, too, was a good Christian girl. Mother and dad adored Beth every bit as much as I did. I couldn't wait to marry Elizabeth and bring her to the Black Diamond. Beth fit into the Jarrett family like a hand fits a glove.

"When Beth started losing weight and looking peaked, she blamed it on semester tests. I wanted her to see a doctor, but she said she couldn't afford it. She was working her way through school. *I* could afford it. But Beth was fiercely independent. She wouldn't accept anything of value from me, not until after we were married. Finally, at my insistence, Beth saw a doctor. It wasn't semester tests. It was leukemia. Dad spared no expense in getting Beth the best treatment. Her family and ours, and all our friends prayed for a cure, at least for a remission. Within six months Beth was 'called to her Maker.'" Jared's voice was caustic. "I ask you—what kind of Maker recalls a twenty-one-year-old girl, with a whole life ahead of her, as if she were some kind of factory reject?" Jared's eyes were glazed with grief.

"Then on top of that, we lost Jenetia. She and I were very close. I loved Jen dearly. Since then, I've quit bothering to love. I may marry, but I promise you—when I do—it certainly won't be for love."

"I see," Kathy said softly.

Jared hadn't missed the pain in Kathy's blue eyes when he admitted he was going to marry Alana. He knew he had shattered her romantic daydreams—fantasies he himself had occasionally entertained. He braced himself to be callous. It was better for her to suffer a few moments of realistic heartbreak than to suffer through deluding daydreams.

"Please don't repeat what I've told you about my plans to marry Alana," Jared instructed when he parked in front of the Black Diamond headquarters. "Ours won't be a marriage made in heaven, but socially it will be convenient. And, with a bit of luck, perhaps even somewhat satisfying."

Jared felt needlessly cruel as he witnessed the soft glow of love in Kathy's gentle eyes flicker, fade, then all but die with his words. What he saw in her face gave him almost physical agony. He had hurt her deeply. But what Kathy did not know was that at that moment Jared was suffering, too. Only because he loved her as he did could he willingly, wholeheartedly thrust her into Guy's caring arms. Jared trusted Guy Armitage with everything he had—his Ranch —his wealth—even with the woman he loved, but dared not possess as his own.

"I'm sorry if I've been rough on you," Jared said quietly as they walked toward the house. "I shouldn't have called you a fool. I've no more right to belittle your beliefs than you have to ridicule mine. Can I still consider you a friend?"

"Yes." Kathy's agreement was faint.

"Good," Jared said. He squared his shoulders, and his voice held the leaden ring of finality.

Mrs. Jarrett met them at the front door. "I thought I heard you come home," she said. "Jared, Alana is on the telephone. You can take the call in the office."

Jared nodded and strode down the hall. Mrs. Jarrett gave Kathy a bright smile, then saw the distraught look on the girl's pretty face.

"Did you have an enjoyable day?" she asked.

126

Kathy attempted a smile. "Pleasant enough. But I'm very tired."

She stammered her excuses and fled to her private quarters, closing the door just as the tears began to fall.

Jared had called her a fool, then apologized, saying he was wrong. But she *had* been a fool. A fool to love him. A fool to surrender to the human longings of her heart. Oatie was wrong. Wrong! If Jared had ever loved her, he wouldn't have spoken to her as he had. Or tried his own hand at matchmaking—hardly the actions of the bitterly jealous man Oatie claimed him to be.

Kathy knew without doubt that the time had come to leave the Black Diamond Ranch, and *soon*—before the pain became too much to bear. With Margot's appraisal by the specialist several weeks away, and with arrangements for her enrollment in a local school in the fall, Kathy's services were no longer really needed.

The next day, and the next, Kathy put off making her move known. Her attachment for all her new friends made it easy to delay leaving the Black Diamond.

Following the conversation on the way back from the auction, Jared avoided Kathy, just as carefully as she avoided him. Hard as she had tried to banish the feelings in her heart, she had failed.

Even after all he had said, she was still attracted to Jared, still loved him. But Jared Jarrett was everything she did *not* need in a husband. It was just as well he was going to marry Alana. Then she would be forced to forget him.

By the first week of August, Kathy spoke to Mrs. Jarrett. "Now that things are progressing so well with Margot," she said, one day when they were alone, "I think it's time for me to move on."

Mrs. Jarrett was heartbroken, but she had not missed the inner turmoil Kathy had experienced since the day of the auction. She could only guess at the reason.

"We hate to have you go, but I trust you to do whatever is right. We're going to miss you. You're one of us now, you know!" There were tears in her eyes.

127

Mrs. Jarrett walked with Kathy to the doorway of the office. Jared was leaving his office with Alana beside him, when they met in the hallway.

"Kathy's leaving us," Mrs. Jarrett announced. Jared stopped short and gave the girl a searching glance.

"How soon?" he asked carefully.

She avoided his eyes. "Very soon. As soon as I can make all the arrangements."

"You're leaving?" Alana wailed. "But you *can't!* Jared Jarrett—don't you *dare* allow her to leave before my party. She promised me she'd be there!"

"I—I did?" Kathy murmured.

Alana smiled. "You bet you did. You promised me that you and Guy would both be there, and I'm going to hold you to it. I'm going to be very offended if you skip out just before my birthday party."

"Why don't you stay, Kathy?" Mrs. Jarrett asked. "I can't attend Alana's party because of an engagement of long standing. Margot's going. Guy could take you both. Having you there would be a favor to me."

Kathy felt drained. In the face of Mrs. Jarrett's request, she had no defense. But Alana Fontaine's party was the last place in the world she wanted to be. It would be sheer agony to witness Jared Jarett commit himself to a marriage without love to a woman who would give herself to him in exchange for the Jarrett name and wealth.

"I have nothing to wear," Kathy said weakly. "The party is formal, I know, and I'm afraid I have nothing suitable."

While it was true, the words sounded limp, the excuse artificial, even to Kathy' ears, and she saw that Alana wasn't about to accept it.

"Anything you wore would be in perfect taste, Kathy," she insisted. "Or . . ." Alana's eyes narrowed. "We could find something in town." Alana smiled teasingly up at Jared.

"You're right, pet." He picked up the cue. "We owe Miss Newby a bonus. Take Kathy and treat her to a gown at your mother's boutique. Put it on my charge account.''

Alana untwined her fingers from Jared's and clapped her hands with delight.

"Do you hear that, Kathy? We'll go this very afternoon,'' Alana decided. "You must look ravishing at my party. Mustn't she, Jared?''

"Whatever you say, pet,'' Jared agreed indulgently.

With encouragement from Mrs. Jarrett, Kathy got her purse, freshened her make-up, and left for town with Alana. Alana pulled her sportscar to a stop in front of the boutique. As the girls entered through a canopied door, Alana brushed a kiss across her mother's cheek, and introduced Kathy.

"Mother, I want something smashing for my friend. Pick out a few gowns, would you, dear?''

Mrs. Fontaine asked Kathy's size, then selected several full-length gowns from the rack, while Alana showed her to a dressing room.

"This one is definitely out!'' Alana flung a gown from her mother's left arm over the right. "It's too similar to the gown I'm wearing.'' As she dug through the various folds of material, she frowned. "These will do for a start. We've got to find something stupendous—and hang the cost— Jared's picking up the tab.'' She winked. "He can afford it!''

Kathy tried on dress after dress as Mrs. Fontaine searched through the racks of the store for even more creations.

"These dresses just won't do, mother!'' Alana cried, showing growing impatience. "Don't you have some others?''

"Lani, there's nothing wrong with these—''

"I said they wouldn't *do*!'' Alana interrupted.

After Alana rejected at least a dozen gowns, Kathy realized that the only ones she had approved were totally wrong for her.

"I think you should get the chartreuse gown,'' Alana said, picking up the daringly low-cut, filmy green gown with a long, swirling skirt of tiny pleats. Having tried it on at Alana's insistence, Kathy knew that the dress suited her even less than the others. It showed too much flesh, and the garish color dulled her creamy ivory skin and detracted from the brilliant blue of her eyes.

"I don't think so," Kathy spoke up. "It's a lovely gown—but not right for me. And it's terribly expensive."

"Who cares about the cost?" Alana asked airily. "You're not paying."

"I'm sorry. It's just not for me. I'd like to see the light blue dress, Mrs. Fontaine."

"The crepe with the balloon sleeves and jeweled cuffs?"

"That's the one!"

"A good choice," Mrs. Fontaine agreed. "It looked lovely on you."

"Oh, mother, it did not! It made her look like some dewy-eyed school girl—not a grown woman! Anyway, it's a rag compared with the green one. It only costs half as much."

"I like it. It's the one I'm going to buy . . . and with my own money."

Alana was aghast. "Jared will have a fit," she warned. "He said to put it on his account, and he doesn't like it when people override his instructions."

"That's too bad," Kathy murmured. "I won't accept anything else from him. The Jarretts have been most generous as it is."

"Here's the blue gown. Would you like to try it on again?"

"There's no need," Kathy said. "It fits perfectly. I'll take it."

"I'll box it up right away." Alana gave her mother a withering look.

In the car, Alana impatiently brushed her auburn hair from her oval face.

"You disappointed me, Kathy. You won't look your best in that dress, I can assure you."

Kathy sensed Alana was more piqued than hurt. She, like Jared, was accustomed to having her way.

"It will be my mistake, then, and I'll live with it."

"And my friends at the party will look at you and think—oh, forget it!" Alana sighed and sped toward the Ranch.

On the ten-mile drive, Kathy understood why Alana insisted she stay for the party. It was because Alana, with a woman's intuition perhaps, knew Kathy's true feelings for Jared. It would give her perverse satisfaction to witness Kathy's heartbreak as the engagement became official. Alana was not above gloating over her good fortune in winning the man Kathy loved—but could never possess.

By the time they arrived at the Black Diamond, Alana no longer bothered to conceal her anger. Alana was not lying when she swore she wanted Kathy at her party. She had wanted her there, looking sallow in the chartreuse gown, and feeling terribly out of place. It irked Alana that instead, Kathy would be the picture of confidence, looking radiant, wrecking her carefully laid plans.

It doesn't matter! Alana thought angrily as she gunned the car, gravel spewing from beneath her tires. *So what if Jared loves that prim little fool? He'd never marry her—because he's going to marry me—and everyone knows it!*

At her party, Alana vowed, as she extended her left hand to accept the Jarrett ring from Jared, and all the prestige, the social position, and the untold wealth that accompanied it, she would stare straight into those innocent blue eyes and watch love die. Kathy Newby was not the kind of girl who would ever let herself love a man who belonged to another woman.

CHAPTER 12

"How do I look?"

Margot whirled into Kathy's room on the night of Alana's party, wearing a pale pink dress with a long, full skirt that swished softly around her slim legs as she walked. Her tanned skin glowed; her eyes danced.

"How do you look?" Kathy asked. "Like a dream!"

Margot frowned. "You're not just saying that to be nice?" Margot scrutinized her face reflected in the mirror.

"You bet I mean it, cutie! You'll have all the young fellows tripping over you all night, wanting to dance."

"You, too!" Margot said. "I love, love, *love* that dress on you!"

"Thanks," Kathy grinned. "I do, too."

"Ready to go?" Kathy asked, when Guy called to them from the foyer below.

Frowning, Margot sighed. "No, I'm not. I'd much rather stay home."

Kathy smiled at Margot's candor. "Me, too, to be honest," she sighed. "We must go, though, for Jared's sake—and your mother's."

"I know," Margot groaned and reluctantly got to her

feet. "Boy, is she lucky she had a good reason to get out of this party. I wish *I* had a good reason not to go."

I wish I did, too, Kathy thought.

It was going to be a difficult evening for both of them. When Jared and Alana announced their engagement, Kathy would be expected to express a joy she did not feel, hiding her true emotions as the embers of love that yet remained in her heart grew cool as ashes.

Guy gave a low wolf-whistle when Kathy and Margot descended the stairs to the foyer.

"Who is the whistle for, Guy?" Margot demanded to know. He winked at her.

"For both of you, sweetheart," he said, although he had eyes only for Kathy.

Margot hurried ahead of them to Guy's car. Guy caught Kathy's hand and squeezed it encouragingly.

"You don't have to look so overjoyed at going to the party with me, dear lady," Guy said lightly.

Kathy gave him a level look. "Pardon my flippancy, kind sir, but you don't appear the picture of joviality yourself."

"Pity we can't be happy for Jared tonight, instead of feeling as we do."

The crowd at the Old Mill Inn was lively. Rippling laughter floated on the air as an excellent dance band played. Stylishly dressed couples swayed on the dance floor. Jared and Alana circulated among their guests. Alana was ravishing in a long white gown with a slit that revealed her shapely thigh as she walked. The dress was fastened over one bare shoulder with a large emerald brooch. The silken material clung to Alana's figure, revealing her every inch a desirable woman. Jared was tanned and dashing in a white tuxedo that emphasized his dark good looks.

Kathy's heart ached at the sight of him, and she wrenched her eyes away. She smiled at Margot when the young girl said she was going to join a group of younger guests.

"Care to dance?" Guy asked, not waiting for Kathy's answer as he took her hand and led her onto the dance floor.

They moved in time to the romantic melodies. Kathy appreciated the protective strength of Guy's presence, the tenderness in his hazel eyes.

She looked at Guy as if she were seeing him anew, and she remembered Jared's words. Confusing thoughts enveloped her when she thought about all a Christian man like Guy had to offer a wife, compared to what an unbeliever like Jared would demand.

"A penny for your thoughts, Kath," Guy whispered in her ear, his breath soft against her cheek.

Kathy arched her back and looked into his eyes, momentarily wondering if he had guessed her thoughts. She decided, with relief, that he had not.

"Cheapskate!" she whispered teasingly. "My thoughts are worth at *least* a half-dollar!"

Guy chuckled. "So are Alana's, judging by the evil looks she's been casting in your direction all night."

Kathy stiffened. "At me?"

Guy nodded. "Jealousy has been flashing constantly in those green, green eyes. I'm not the only one here who knows you're the most beautiful woman in the room. Alana knows it, too, and she doesn't like it one bit."

Helplessly Kathy's gaze followed Guy's. Just then, Jared looked up, caught their attention and smiled, bidding them over.

"We'd better go pay our respects to the birthday girl," Guy said.

Hand-in-hand, Guy and Kathy strolled across the crowded room to join the circle of guests clustered around Jared and Alana. Kathy's grip tightened on Guy's hand as they drew near. He smiled down into her miserable blue eyes.

"Buck up," he ordered under his breath. She gave him a thin smile.

"Guy," Jared acknowledged when they stepped up.

The two men exchanged a long look. At the mutual understanding that passed between them, Jared smiled. Guy remained grim.

"Jared," he nodded.

In Guy's heart, he wanted to call his handsome employer every kind of fool. Couldn't Jared see what he was doing? The mistake he was making? Or did Jared know, but stubbornly plan to go ahead anyway?

"Kathy—hello," Jared said quietly.

His eyes swept over her, not missing a detail. For a moment his resolve wavered as he drank in her heartstopping beauty—a beauty of freshness and innocence, with no worldly hardness around the edges. Jared's gaze lingered a moment too long. He ripped his eyes away as Kathy spoke.

"Good evening, Jared . . ."

Alana turned, demanding Jared's attention. She pretended momentarily not to have noticed Guy and Kathy. When she turned to them, her green eyes widened with surprised delight.

"Hello, there! Are you enjoying my party?"

"Yes," Guy answered for both of them.

Alana cocked an eyebrow. "You can't be enjoying it very much. You don't have anything to drink." Her brow dipped into a frown.

"We didn't want anything to drink, thanks," Guy said. "We've been dancing. The band is excellent."

Alana tossed her head and patted Jared's forearm. "The band had better be good for what Jared's paying them. I'm going to signal a waiter. You two *must* have something to drink. If you've been dancing, you must be *parched*!"

Kathy had noticed that most of the couples were sipping mixed drinks. "I'm sorry, Alana, I don't drink," she said softly. "Liquor, that is." She hoped she didn't sound stuffy and judgmental.

Alana wrinkled her nose. "Quite all right. I knew some of Jared's family would be here. And the Jarretts are notorious teetotalers. I had fruit punch made up. I'll get you both some."

Alana darted away before either Guy or Kathy could object. A moment later she returned with two frosty glasses of frothy red fruit punch.

136

"Here you are, Guy," Alana said, smiling as she placed the icy glass in his hand. "And Kathy . . ." Alana took a step toward her, hooked her high heel in the carpeting, and fell forward, screeching with alarm.

An anguished cry escaped Kathy. She jumped back, but it was too late. The icy punch sprayed through the air, soaking the sheer blue fabric on contact, turning the bodice of Kathy's dress a mottled purple and randomly casting violet splotches on the skirt. Kathy stared down at her stained dress and resisted the urge to cry.

"Your dress, Kathy! It's ruined!" Alana wailed. "Oh, I'm so sorry! It was so clumsy of me. Can you ever forgive me?"

"It's all right, Alana," Kathy said, praying for control. She knew that this was another of Alana's "accidents," probably planned well in advance, and staged to perfection. Alana would love nothing more than Kathy's losing her composure in front of the guests.

Guy squeezed Kathy's hand. She raised her eyes to Alana's. The anger was gone, replaced by acceptance and serenity.

"It's all right, Alana. Really. Accidents happen."

Alana shook her head. "No, it's not all right! I ruined your dress. I'll pay for it. We'll get her a new dress, won't we, Jared?"

"Of course," he replied.

Jared's words seemed distant, remote, as if he were scarcely aware of what was occurring at the moment.

Alana bubbled on. "I'll see if mother can't find a duplicate in stock. It's the least I can do after spoiling your gown, as well as the whole evening for you. Poor thing, you're soaked to the skin. You can't stay here like that. Guy will have to take you home." Alana's eyes glittered with triumph.

"You don't mind, do you, Guy?" Alana asked lightly. "Don't worry about leaving Margot. We'll find someone to take her home after the party."

"Let's go, Kath," Guy said. His voice was like steel. Kathy knew he hadn't been fooled by Alana's act, either.

She took a step toward the door with Guy, when a firm grip on her shoulder halted her. She turned back to stare into the eyes of Jared Jarrett—fury sparking behind the calm gray facade.

"Stay and enjoy the party, Guy. Watch out for my sister. I'm taking Kathy to the Ranch."

"Will do, Boss," Guy replied, recognizing the words as an order, not a request.

Before Kathy could fully comprehend what was happening, Jared ushered her from the Inn as surprised guests stared after them. Alana was the first to regain her composure. She followed them to the Club entrance.

"Hurry back, darling," she called.

Jared didn't look in her direction. His lips were a thin, angry line. Alana cast a frightened glance as he sped into the night with Kathy Newby. Then she returned to her guests, an aura of confidence masking her fear.

Kathy peeked at Jared's face, silhouetted in the soft light of the dash. His features were now set in an unfathomable expression. Jared shifted gears violently, tearing down the road at breakneck speed. Kathy was too frightened to protest.

As Jared swung the Jaguar onto the Ranch drive, she finally found her voice. "You should have let Guy bring me home. Alana must be humiliated."

"That's too bad. I wanted to bring you back myself," he said shortly. "If I hadn't wanted to attend to you personally, I could have easily delegated the task to Guy. As for Alana," he laughed mirthlessly, "she heaped her own humiliation upon herself with another little . . . *accident*. She seems to be accident-prone when she's around you."

"Just let me out at the walk," Kathy suggested. "I'll find my own way in, and you can return to the party."

"I'm not going back."

"But you have to!" Kathy thought of Alana's birthday surprise. The Jarrett ring. The plans for their engagement.

"No, I do *not* have to return. I've seen quite enough of Alana's phony friends to last a lifetime."

"Alana will think it's my fault you're not back. She'll blame me," Kathy argued.

"It *is* your fault," Jared said lightly. "I can't return to Alana, Kathy. I know I told you I was going to marry her, but I hadn't asked her yet, and I know now that I never will. Forget whatever I said about love, and marriages of convenience. I knew tonight that I couldn't sell myself short and marry Alana. I'm a businessman, Kathy, but I'm a person, too. I could never settle for a relationship that dishonest. I want more. I want everything—or nothing at all!"

"Everything?" Kathy asked, dazed.

"Everything. I love you, Kath, and I know you love me. No woman, especially not a woman like you, would ever kiss a man the way you kissed me if you didn't feel something. I tried to forget you, tried to push you off on Guy. But I'm ready to face up to it. I love you, and I must have you." Jared fumbled in the pocket of his tuxedo for the ring. Without asking, he took Kathy's hand and slipped it on her finger. She stared at her left hand, stared at Jared. She felt as if she were falling off a high, high cliff, unable to stop herself, holding her breath as she anticipated the bottom.

"There! I've said it and I'll say it again: I love you, Kathy Newby—wildly, passionately, desperately, blindly. I need you. I've known it since the moment we first met."

"Jared . . ."

When he swept her into his arms, Kathy yielded willingly to his kisses, his caresses. The confusing thoughts were tumbling in her head, but her body responded gladly to Jared's ardor. He was the first to pull away, his breathing ragged, his hands trembling.

"We'd better get you in the house," he said, his voice hoarse with emotion. "I'm warning you—I'm an impatient man. So we'd better set the date *soon*!"

Kathy looked up at him. Her lips moved but no sound came out. Tears stung her eyes as Jared's words forced her back to reality and out of the dream world of his embrace.

"When can we be married, my darling?" he urged.

Her voice shook as she turned away. "We can't get married, Jared. I can't accept your proposal. I'm so sorry . . . but I can't."

Jared grasped Kathy's wrist and refused to let her turn away. His eyes bored into hers.

"Can't?" The word was strangled. "Can't? Why not? Have you already promised Guy?"

"No."

Jared sagged with relief. "Then why not? Tell me, Kathy! What could possibly be standing in our way—"

"You're not a Christian, Jared."

Her words, spoken reluctantly, were as soft and gentle as the evening breeze, but they struck Jared with a resounding blow. His senses reeled with disbelief.

"You can't be serious!"

"I'm sorry; I am serious," she wept. "I promised myself long ago I'd never marry a man who wasn't committed to Jesus Christ, as I am. That's why I can't marry you, Jared, even though I do love you—with all my heart." She was sobbing brokenly.

"I can't believe you'd let religion stand in the way of happiness," Jared glowered. "If so, then you're a bigger fool than I ever thought you to be."

Kathy's sobs subsided. "It seems calling me a fool has become quite a habit with you. I'll gladly be a fool for the Lord, but I won't be a fool for you."

Jared sighed. "Kath . . . Kathy—you are completely mystifying! Forgive me, but I'm not used to giving in to other people, darling. If it will make you happy, I'll go to church with you. I'll give, and give generously to any Christian cause or charity you would like to support. You can raise our children in any way you wish; there will be no objections from me."

Kathy knew that Jared was utterly sincere in his offers. But all of them put together were still not enough.

"Your going to church would make us all very happy, Jared, but church attendance isn't what being a Christian means. Christianity isn't a going-through-the-motions thing. It's a commitment to a person—Jesus Christ—who will take over and guide your life. It means trusting in Him, not in yourself, with *all* your gifts and abilities.''

"After all I've offered you—you're *still* turning me down?" Jared asked, knowing the answer was already written on Kathy's face.

"We're not the same kind of people, Jared. Don't you see? You want me now, and I want and love you. But what about the future? You would get tired of going to church. You'd come to resent what Jesus Christ means to me! I'd cramp your style. You say you love me now, and perhaps you do, but someday, Jared, unless you became the Christian husband I need you to be, you'd very likely come to . . . hate me.''

Jared swore savagely. "Never! That's not true! I want you now and I'll want you forever. The same way you want me.''

Jared grabbed Kathy, forced her into his arms, and kissed her roughly, demanding that she respond to him, to answer his passion with her own. He released her, but kept a grip on her shoulders, his eyes probing hers.

"Now,'' he said in a low voice, "tell me you don't want me. Deny it, *now*!''

"I won't deny it,'' Kathy said softly. "I do want you, but that's not enough.''

"Well!'' Jared's breath escaped in a whistling sigh. "I'm sorry! Somehow I've always thought of myself as a decent, hardworking person. No matter what I offer, it doesn't seem good enough for you. I'm sorry I'm so sadly lacking in your eyes, Miss Newby.'' Jared's voice was cold. "And I have my doubts that any man will ever live up to the requirements you've set. I thought you were the perfect woman, but, in your own way, you're every bit as flawed as Alana!''

Jared's words hurt as he intended them to. Kathy didn't call out to him. She watched his car roar past the gates, and her heart broke. She had lost him . . .

That night, she prayed that her pain would not be without purpose. Without even removing the stained gown, Kathy sank to the bed, buried her face in the crook of her arm, and wept. She wept for Jared, and for their love that was not to be. She could not compromise her beliefs for anyone. Not even for Jared Jarrett.

CHAPTER 13

KATHY'S EYES FELT gritty from tears when she dressed the next morning, quickly packed her belongings, and patted cool water on her face, hoping it would undo some of the ravage caused by her sleepless night. As she left her room, she prayed for the courage to do what had to be done.

Oatie was the only one up when Kathy slipped past the kitchen. She wasn't ready for a confrontation with the inquisitive cook before she had composed herself.

Looking toward the parking area, Kathy was relieved to see Mrs. Jarrett's Lincoln in its slot. Kathy made her way to the ell, hoping Victoria Jarrett was in her office and free to talk.

"Kathy—so good to see you!" she welcomed. "Come in!"

"Did you have a nice trip, Mrs. Jarrett?"

"Splendid," she replied, "although I'll be glad when my calendar clears up some. Now that I'm needed at home," she smiled, "I'm trying to be more selective of the groups and charities I endorse with my time as well as my money."

"I'd like to discuss something important."

"Of course."

Kathy closed the door and seated herself. Mrs. Jarrett had suspected, by the look on Kathy's face, that it was a serious matter.

She spoke quickly. "I hate to give such short notice, but I want to leave right away . . . today."

The older woman remained silent for a long moment. She had already heard the gossip about the fiasco at the Old Mill Inn when she had her car serviced at the station in town before proceeding to the Ranch. It seemed the whole area was buzzing with the news that Jared had left Alana standing alone at her party, and the expected engagement had not been announced. Jared's Jaguar was not in the lot when Mrs. Jarrett returned that morning. He was probably driving aimlessly, or was holed up in some motel or tourist cabin somewhere, thinking.

"You want to leave because of Jared." It was a statement, not a question.

Kathy nodded. Fresh tears started, but she willed them away.

"Jared asked you to marry him last night, didn't he?" Mrs. Jarrett asked gently.

Kathy nodded miserably, reaching into her pocket for the ring she had forgotten to return in the heat of their argument. She placed the Jarrett ring between them on the desk.

"And you turned him down . . ."

"I had to."

Mrs. Jarrett smiled. Her voice was without reproach. "I know you did, dear. And I understand why, although nothing could have made me happier than to welcome you to the Black Diamond as Jared's bride. Time heals all wounds, Kathy. You'll recover. I did."

Kathy gave Mrs. Jarrett a questioning look. Her expression was faraway and dreamy, almost amused, although Kathy saw there a faint trace of hurt at the memory.

"Yes, dear Kathy, I *do* understand the agony you're going through. I went through it myself thirty-eight years ago when I was a twenty-year-old girl wildly in love with a

144

handsome young fellow from one of the best families in Belle Fourche. He had as much money as my own family. Everyone expected we would get married. Frankly, I did consider it. I was very tempted. But we were from two different worlds. When he did ask me to marry him, after much soul searching, Kathy, I did just what you've done. I turned my young man down—for the same reasons. It almost broke my heart, but I trusted that the right man would eventually be there for me.

"Two years later, I met Thomas Jarrett. In a short time we were married and he brought me home to the Black Diamond. Waiting for a Christian man was a choice I've never regretted for a moment. Tom and I had a beautiful life together because the source of our love was Jesus Christ. You are hurting now, Kathy, but trust me, you made the right decision." Kathy smiled through her unshed tears, unable to speak. "I do regret very much losing you as an employee, dear, but I know that we'll never lose you as a friend. . . . Now, I know you want to leave, and quickly. I'll issue your paycheck. I don't know what plans Guy has for the day, but I'm sure nothing that can't be postponed long enough for him to drive you to the airport. Have you any idea where you'll be going?"

"Yes," Kathy said, thinking of the open invitation at Trish Nobel's home in Kansas City.

"Then goodbye, Kathy. And God bless you."

Kathy returned to her room as Mrs. Jarrett reached for the telephone . . .

Minutes later Kathy carried her bags downstairs, dreading the farewells with Mrs. Otis and Margot.

Oatie, still unaware of the happenings of the night before, assumed Kathy would be back shortly. She responded with a warning that Kathy had better not return to her kitchen all skin and bones.

"I won't—I promise!" she laughed.

Guy arrived at the front door. His face was grim, but his eyes were tender and understanding.

"Margot's out back. By the pool," he murmured, as he loaded her luggage.

Kathy swallowed hard and nodded. The good-bye to Oatie had been easy; the encounter with Margot would not be.

She found Margot huddled on the patio near the pool, crying, staring unseeingly over the pastures of the Black Diamond as tears rolled steadily down her softly curving cheeks. Margot avoided looking at Kathy when she approached.

"Margot," she spoke softly, hoping for control. "I have to leave now."

"So I heard." Margot swiped at tears trailing down her cheeks. She convulsed with a sob. "Oh, Kathy, can't you stay?" she cried.

Kathy wavered, but only for an instant. "No, Margot, I can't stay, much as I would like to. Someday, honey, when you're older, perhaps you'll understand why I have to leave." Margot threw herself into Kathy's arms. "It's not like we'll never see each other again," she gave Margot a firm hug. "I'll try to come back and visit you . . . someday. And you can come visit me."

Margot was sobbing when Kathy left her. Her own eyes were damp and she struggled for control.

"Buck up, ol' buddy," Guy drawled. Kathy didn't dare look at him. It was like a wrenching physical pain to leave the Black Diamond Ranch and the people she had grown to love. "Ready to go?" he asked, as he opened the door to the green station wagon.

When Kathy didn't answer, Guy regarded her in silence. From the set of her chin, Guy knew she was determined to leave, but he wasn't sure if he should let her go. Guy took his seat behind the steering sheel, but made no move to start the ignition.

"Are you positive that leaving—running away—is the right thing to do?" Kathy shrugged, unable to answer. "Hey," Guy said softly. "I know Jared Jarrett. He can be a beast when he's riled. I can imagine what he said to you, but basically, he's a good guy. He'll be around to apologize when he comes back—and he'll mean it. Jared gets mad, then goes off for a few hours, sometimes even a few days, gets his head together, and comes back. Don't leave, Kathy, without thinking things through! I know Jared, Kath, and he loves you. Very, very much. He walked out on you and I know it had to hurt, but Jared cares for you. I promise you—he'll be back.''

Kathy lifted her eyes. Guy saw then she was quietly crying.

"Jared may come back. But when he does, I won't be here.''

"All right,'' Guy said. "As long as you know what you're doing.''

Guy started the car, backed away from the Ranch headquarters, and quickly drove down the lane. Sensing that Kathy didn't want to run into Jared, Guy turned off the highway and took an alternate route to the airport. With every mile, Kathy seemed to be regaining strength.

When they neared the airport, she dreaded the parting with Guy, not knowing when she'd see him again. Tears seemed too close to the surface. Kathy didn't want Guy to remember her with tears streaming down her cheeks. She prayed for the grace and strength to hang on for a few minutes longer.

Guy parked in the terminal lot, lifted Kathy's bags from the rear, and started toward the building. She reached out to take them from him.

"Please, Guy, leave me right here. Don't go in with me. It'll be easier for both of us if we make it a quick good-bye now, rather than prolong the agony until my plane leaves.''

"Whatever you want, love,'' Guy said softly.

"Good-bye, Guy,'' Kathy whispered. She slipped into his arms to receive his hug and farewell kiss. Just as quickly she slipped away again, not trusting herself to hold back the tears much longer.

"Everything will turn out for you, Kathy,'' Guy's voice was confident. "I'm not going to say good-bye to you. I'll wait, instead, until we say hello again.''

Then he was gone and Kathy hurried into the terminal to make the arrangements that would take her far, far away from the Black Diamond Ranch.

She went directly to the ticket agent and booked passage for Kansas City on a standby basis. She had hoped for a confirmed ticket, but the agent explained that the flights were overbooked. There would be only a short wait until the next departure.

Kathy checked her luggage, went to the cafeteria for a bite to eat, and bought a magazine to read while she waited the two hours for her flight to depart.

When it was time for the jet to land and refuel before taking off for Kansas City, Kathy, feeling impatient, went to the observation window that was filling fast with other people scanning the sky for incoming crafts.

The orange wind vane stood out in the breeze. Several light airplanes, privately owned craft, landed and took off. Kathy started to turn away from the window when a small blue-and-white airplane touched down on the runway. It looked hauntingly familiar.

As the small, incoming jet landed, the intercommunications system blared with flight numbers and information, signaling that the flight to Kansas City was soon to depart. Kathy picked up her hand luggage and moved into the security line. She stepped up to the security stall where the somber-faced officer was giving boarding passangers a practiced look, before placing their carry-on luggage through the electronic eye. She handed the guard her case and handbag. He motioned her through the stall.

"Kathy—*stop*!"

At the sound of her name, she halted. She turned to see Jared half-running toward her. The guard grew impatient as Kathy froze, blocking the line, to stare at Jared.

"Hurry up, Miss! It's too late now for good-byes. The airplane is getting ready to leave. These passengers need to get through!"

"Kathy!" Jared leaned over the steel railing. He touched her arm. "Wait—just a minute—it's all I ask. Please!"

Jared's eyes seemed desperate, but subdued, pleading instead of commanding.

"Jared, my flight is about to leave. If I miss it—"

"If you still want to leave, after you hear what I have to say, I'll fly you anywhere you want to go. I promise you. Now please, leave the line and talk to me, Kathy. It's very important."

With an apologetic smile, she collected her case and walked against the press of passengers moving through the security station, to meet Jared. He took her arm, leading her away from the milling crowd.

"Oh . . . Kathy," Jared's eyes were soft, his voice very gentle. "Thank God, I got here in time! When Guy got back with the station wagon and told me he'd left you at the airport, I'd just returned to the Ranch myself. I had come back to see you, to tell you my news. Today I kept that promise I made to mother. Thinking about your disappearing without a trace into a big city gave me the courage I needed to pilot an airplane again."

She waited, unable to speak, as the torrent of words continued to pour from Jared.

"I was furious when I left you last night, Kathy—wild with frustration and hurt. I couldn't comprehend how the woman I loved more than life could turn me down in favor of a God, a Being that couldn't be touched, seen, heard . . .

"While I drove, I did a lot of thinking about my childhood, my parents, but most of all, about myself—the life I've lived. I was raised to go to church, but it meant little to me. After going away to the university, it was an easy habit to break. After Leila, I was bitter. Then, with Beth, I started attending church again, but only to make her happy, not because I truly wanted to.

"After Beth died, I went into the Navy. I was stationed as a pilot on an aircraft carrier in the Mediterranean. I traveled a great deal when I was overseas. I saw a lot of cultures, experienced foreign customs, and saw so many religions that I began to doubt *all* of them. How could I be sure that mother and her Christian beliefs were right when there were so many religions, and what you personally believed seemed dictated by what family you happened to have been born into? It was impossible for me to believe in a God that all the religions of the world couldn't even agree on."

Words failed miserably, Jared thought, as he tried to explain that, while he had not known before, he knew now that there *was* a God, and that Jesus Christ, God made Man, cared about Jared Jarrett.

In Kathy's tender eyes, Jared saw that further words were unnecessary. He didn't have to convince her because she already understood, and understood well, what he was trying to say. She shared his newfound beliefs just as Jared knew that Kathy would share everything in the future.

"I turned my back on the Lord," Jared said. "He knocked on my heart a great many times and I hardened it against Him. Human nature pridefully got in the way. I told myself that I could run my life the way I wanted without consulting anyone. Not even Him. So, Katherine Newby, I was the fool . . . not you." Jared paused. "You weren't sent to the Ranch without a purpose. You served His purpose well. You were the vessel He used to bring the Jarrett family back together. Our family is one with a long Christian tradition, Kathy, until Margot and I threatened to ruin it. Now I'm asking you to be my wife, and to help me—and our children—carry on that tradition of faith."

Kathy's heart swelled with joy, and overflowed in grateful prayers of praise and thanksgiving. She flew into Jared's waiting arms.

"Jared—yes! Oh, *yes!*"

He buried his face in Kathy's neck, holding her as if he'd never let her go. Happily she lifted her lips to his, not caring if the whole world looked on. Let them see the beginning that would have no end. This love would endure. This commitment was forever. Kathy exulted in the knowledge that she had stood firm in her beliefs—had kept love's sweet promise.

Jared broke away. Reaching into his pocket, he brought forth a small case. Inside was the Jarrett ring. The rare gems glowed with warmth and promise as Jared held it out to her. This time, he was asking, not demanding, that she accept it and become his wife.

"The Jarrett ring was meant for special women, Kathy —Christian women loved and cherished by Jarrett men."

Kathy held out her hand. Jared slipped the ring on her finger where it would remain until that day when their eldest son chose a strong Christian woman to be his bride.

MEET THE AUTHOR

SUSAN C. FELDHAKE lives with her husband, Steve, and their children on Sow's Ear Acres, the family farm in central Illinois. Her interests include canning garden produce, cooking from original receipes, and keeping pioneer arts alive in a modern world. When she isn't working on her novels, Susan likes to read, play the piano, and spend cozy evenings visiting with friends.

Susan writes, "My husband and I believe that our most priceless possession is our shared faith. It was the realization that many couples take this spiritual dimension of marriage for granted or, worse still, do not consider it at all, that prompted the writing of *Love's Sweet Promise*."

A Letter To Our Readers

Dear Reader:

Pioneering is an exhilarating experience, filled with opportunities for exploring new frontiers. The Zondervan Corporation is proud to be the first major publisher to launch a series of inspirational romances designed to inspire and uplift as well as to provide wholesome entertainment. In order that we might better contribute to your reading enjoyment, we would appreciate your taking a few minutes to respond to the following questions and return to:

> Anne Severance, Editor
> Serenade/Saga Books
> 749 Templeton Drive
> Nashville, Tennessee   37205

1. Did you enjoy reading LOVE'S SWEET PROMISE?

   ☐ Very much. I would like to see more books by this author!
   ☐ Moderately
   ☐ I would have enjoyed it more if _____

2. Please rate the following elements (from 1 to 10):

   ☐ Heroine   ☐ Plot
   ☐ Hero   ☐ Inspirational theme
   ☐ Setting   ☐ Secondary characters

3. Which settings do you prefer?

_____   _____

_____   _____

4. What are some inspirational themes you would like to
   see treated in future Serenade books?

_____   _____

_____   _____

5. What influenced your decision to purchase this book?

   ☐ Cover   ☐ Back cover copy
   ☐ Title   ☐ Friends
   ☐ Publicity   ☐ Other _____

6. Would you be interested in reading other Serenade or
   Serenade Saga Books?

   ☐ Very interested
   ☐ Moderately interested
   ☐ Not interested

7. Please indicate your age range:

   ☐ Under 18   ☐ 25–34   ☐ 46–55
   ☐ 18–24   ☐ 35–45   ☐ Over 55

8. Would you be interested in a Serenade book club? If so,
   please give us your name and address:

   Name _____

   Address _____

   City _____ State _____ Zip _____

Serenade Books are inspirational romances in contemporary settings, designed to bring you a joyful, heart-lifting reading experience.

Other Serenade books available in your local bookstore:

#1 ON WINGS OF LOVE, Elaine L. Schulte
#2 LOVE'S SWEET PROMISE, Susan C. Feldhake
#3 FOR LOVE ALONE, Susan C. Feldhake
#4 LOVE'S LATE SPRING, Lydia Heermann
#5 IN COMES LOVE, Mab Graff Hoover
#6 FOUNTAIN OF LOVE, Velma S. Daniels and Peggy E. King.

Watch for the Serenade/Saga Series, historical inspirational romances, to be released in January, 1984.